noonie's masterpiece

noonie's masterpiece

By
Lisa Railsback

art By
Sarajo Frieden

chronicle books · san francisco

*To Patricia, my mom, who has read everything I've written
since the first grade.*

—Lisa Railsback

*Dedicated to lily belle burk (1992–2009): you will always be
a part of us.*

*To my family, especially my son Miro, and friends: I love you
all dearly. Thanks to Amelia Anderson and Victoria Rock at
Chronicle Books, as well as Lisa Railsback for writing this lovely
book. Lastly, thanks to my agents at Lilla Rogers Studio.*

—Sarajo Frieden

Text © 2010 by Lisa Railsback.
Illustrations © 2010 by Sarajo Frieden.
All rights reserved. No part of this book may be reproduced in any
form without written permission from the publisher.

Library of Congress Cataloging-in-Publication Data
Railsback, Lisa.
Noonie's masterpiece / by Lisa Railsback.
p. cm.
Summary: Upon learning that her deceased mother, an artist, went through a "Purple Period,"
ten-year-old Noonie decides to do the same, hoping that this will bring her archaeologist father
home to see her win a school art contest and that the aunt, uncle, and cousin she lives with will
come to understand her just a little.
ISBN 978-0-8118-6654-5
[1. Artists—Fiction. 2. Eccentrics and eccentricities—Fiction. 3. Family life—Fiction.
4. Fathers and daughters—Fiction. 5. Schools—Fiction. 6. Self-actualization (Psychology)
—Fiction.] I. Title.
PZ7.R1287Noo 2010
[Fic]—dc22
2008026831

Book design by Amelia May Anderson.
Typeset in BodoniEgyptian and American Typewriter.
The illustrations in this book were rendered in pen, ink, and watercolor.

Manufactured by Toppan Leefung, Da Ling Shan Town, Dongguan, China, in November 2009.

10 9 8 7 6 5 4 3 2 1

This product conforms to CPSIA 2008.

Chronicle Books LLC
680 Second Street, San Francisco, California 94107

www.chroniclekids.com

a brilliant artist
must try not
to be afraid

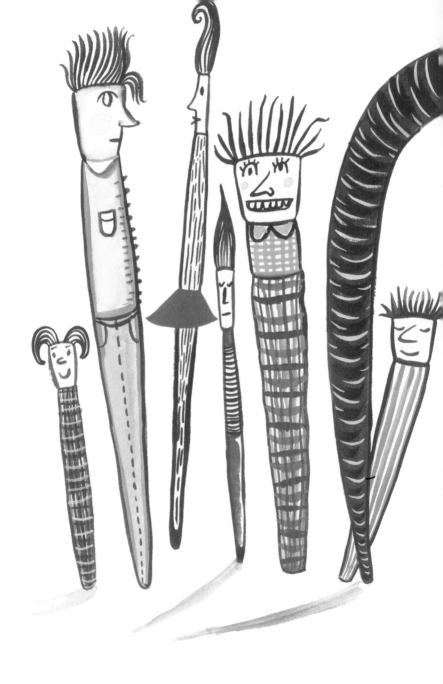

My Horribly Blue Life

chapter one

Dear Art and History People,
My name is Noonie Norton, and I'm a brilliant artist. The only small problem is that I haven't been discovered yet. See, most brilliant artists aren't actually discovered until they're dead, so I thought I should explain my art while I'm still alive. That way there will be no possibility of misinterpretation. Because—well, tomorrow I might be trampled by a herd of kindergartners or I might choke to death on a rotten nut. You never know what can happen to an artist.

   You should definitely take a whole lot of notes because in a hundred years people will want to know everything about me. They'll want to know about my life when I was five years old, and fourteen years old, and twenty-three years old, and thirty years old (if I make it that long). But now I'm ten, so we'll start right here.

My career began like this: I painted my first self-portrait in kindergarten. That was the start of my Blue Period. My mom died, which was the beginning of everything horrible. Then my sad dad, who didn't know what else to do, decided to leave me with Aunt Sylvia and Uncle Ralph. Double horrible.

I was very, very blue. My face was blue, my body was blue, my hair was blue. Not a pretty blue, but a dark, stormy black blue. My mouth was in a jagged blue squiggle from one side of my messy head to the other.

I'm sure my kindergarten teacher, Mr. Pitts, was afraid. He'd probably

never seen a six-year-old paint herself so blue before.
Ordinary kindergartners paint themselves smiling
yellow or cheery pink. He showed my self-portrait to
the principal, who showed it to the school counselor,
who showed it to Aunt Sylvia and Uncle Ralph. Of
course. Then all of them talked and talked—about
me—and decided that I'd probably grow out of
being blue.

I hung that first self-portrait in
the back of my closet with
a thumbtack. I can look
at my blue self whenever
I want. It's good to
remember where you've
been. The beginning
of my Blue Period was
a lousy, rotten time,
and things have been
squiggly blue ever
since.

I still live with
Aunt Sylvia and
Uncle Ralph and my
cousin, Junior. This

would probably be fine if I were a sunny-yellow or a cheery-pink fourth-grader. Unfortunately, my aunt and uncle don't understand brilliant-artist fourth-graders a single bit. Most people don't. My mom would have, of course, if she hadn't died when I was in kindergarten. And my dad? Well, he collects all my work. And any day now he's going to understand just about everything. I'm sure of it.

My dad left me here, with my aunt and uncle, because he was sure I'd be "better off in a real home with a real family." That's exactly what he said. Because, see, his job is doing archaeological digs in all sorts of weird faraway places. He digs up old bones and old pots and stares at old crusty drawings made in caves about a million years ago. He didn't think I would want to be sinking into tar pits, spelunking through caves, traveling all the time—"because, really, how fun can that possibly be for you, Noonie? No regular school? No friends?" That's what he said. But I think it all sounds pretty darn fantastic. I'd rather be living in Timbuktu and riding on a sweaty camel with my dad. I'd rather be just about anywhere but here.

I sent a letter off to him a couple of weeks ago. Another letter.

I drew a picture of my blue self with blue foam gurgling out of my blue mouth. I stuffed it in the envelope and sealed the envelope with Scotch tape. As usual. See, I've sent my dad about a hundred letters almost exactly like this one, all with my very original art inside. It's important to remind him that my art is *much* better than those weird cave drawings. He writes back immediately, and sometimes he even comes home. Pronto. It's worked before.

Last time he came home pronto was when I drew myself with a blue face covered in about a hundred green dots. It was obviously a terrible case of the Moldy Blue Fever from eating Aunt Sylvia's mushy green vegetables. He also came home when I drew myself with an enormous blue head. Definitely Bloated Blue Brain from too much homework. And before that I had the most horrible cases of Blue Bathtime Rot, Blue Flu, and strange, mysterious Blue Warts. All very deadly.

Dear Dad,

I'm afraid that I've caught a very fatal sickness. I'm sure I caught it from Cousin Junior, because he likes to bite. I hate to tell you, but . . . it's a terrible case of the BITING BLUE RABIES. My mouth is foaming nearly all the time. So I think you better come home PRONTO, before it's too late.

Love,
Noonie

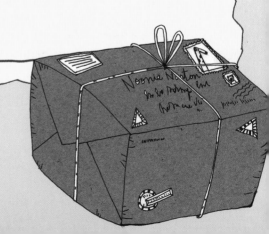

Today after school I ran straight to the mailbox, as always, to see if he'd written back. And guess what? There wasn't just a letter inside, but a package! Sure enough, it was addressed to me: *Noonie Norton*! It had scribbly letters on it in some foreign language and a funny-looking stained stamp.

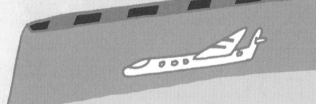

Dear Noonie,

Blue rabies? That does sound serious indeed. I'd love nothing more than to see you PRONTO. Unfortunately, I can't fly home just yet, Noonie. I'll be home very soon, but I have to finish up this work in China. I'm busy analyzing what may be the first bones of the wild yak. I'm also learning how to use chopsticks and I'm being taught calligraphy from a Chinese master.

Thanks for the new blue picture of you. It will be added, of course, to my collection of all your other blue pictures. Did I ever tell you that your mom had a PURPLE PERIOD? For a while she painted just about everything in purple.

Wish I were home with you now.

Love,
Dad

P.S. Will you let your Aunt Sylvia know about your newest illness? Maybe a good healthy medicine, like triple chocolate-chunk ice cream, will help.

P.P.S. I hope these special presents will help, too.

Yak bones? Who really cares about wild grimy old yak bones? And Aunt Sylvia curing me? Hmmph. Even with my favorite ice cream she could never cure me. Well, not the way my dad could. Not really.

But at the very bottom of my package was something much better than a bone or a chopstick. I was afraid to even touch it because everything good gets ruined.

Chinese Hat

It was a purple hat all the way from China! I put it on my head pronto, even though it smelled funny. And of course it fit my head perfectly. Most likely I will never take my purple Chinese hat off ever again. Because inside my new artist hat my dad pinned a napkin.

It wasn't just any ordinary napkin. Oh, no. On one side the napkin said the name of some café in Paris, France. And on the other side was a purple painting by . . . my *mom*! From a long, long time ago. There were purple waves and purple swirls, and in the very center there was a very little picture of my very purple mom. Brilliant.

Art and History People, I've decided that today is the very last day of my Blue Period. Tomorrow my Purple Period will officially begin.

It will be a very important period in my career, and I think you should pay close attention and take a whole lot of notes so there will be no possibility of misinterpretation. Good things will definitely happen in my Purple Period. I'm sure of it. Why? Well, because my mom was purple and because a girl can't be blue forever. Right?

sincerely
Noonie Norton

"wake

chapter two

the Artist's Unusually Unusual Awakening

The first day of my Purple Period started just like this:

Rrrrrrrring!

My alarm went off. Seven o'clock. I knew right away it would be different. It already felt very unusually unusual. Very artistically strange. Even if Aunt Sylvia was hollering outside my door, just like every other morning. "Noonie! Noonie sweetie! Time to wake up! Wakey-wakey!"

Noonie

I decided right then and there,
under my covers, that in my Purple
Period I didn't have to wake up on time.
Everyone knows that most artists sleep all day
and work all night. I didn't have to get dressed
in folded clothes from my drawer or go to
Grover Cleveland Elementary School.

"*Noo-oo-oo-nie!*" sang her voice again, like
a bug biting my ear.

I grumbled. Instead of jumping out of bed, I
leisurely rolled over and snorted like an artist.

Aunt Sylvia's work shoes squeaked across my
bedroom floor.

Squeak-squeak-squeak.

I peeked out and saw her large happy face.
Her perfectly white teeth and her crisp white
dental hygienist outfit almost blinded me.

I pulled my covers back over my head,
hoping that I looked exactly like a mummy or a
voodoo doll.

"Upsy-daisy! Rise and shiny!" chirped Aunt
Sylvia as if this were the shiniest morning ever.

"Upsy-daisy Rise and shiny!"

I didn't answer. I didn't even move a pinky. Silence.

"She must be shocked and amazed," I thought. "She must be able to sense my new purple life."

But then, suddenly, "*Noo-nieeeeee!*" she sang like an opera star. "Sweetie? We don't want to be late, now do we? No, no. There's no time for dillydallying, so let's get ourselves *up* and get dressed for school!"

up! up! up!
up! up!

She squeaked away again, and as she was leaving, I heard her say, "And why are you wearing that funny purple hat in bed, sweetie?"

I sighed. I pulled my covers off and got up. I stomped my foot with artistic temperament. I was absolutely *not* going to put on clean clothes from my drawer. Fortunately, I was already wearing my favorite jeans, with holey knees and scraggly bottoms. I'd slept in them, of course. Artists hate pajamas and always wear their clothes to bed. *If* they even go to bed.

I dug around under my bed and found a wrinkled T-shirt and threw it on. Meanwhile, I tried very hard to ignore the big ugly math book, which was also under my bed, where it had been since the first day of fourth grade. I pushed a pile of dirty clothes over it. Because I definitely didn't need to give a hoot about math. Famous artists hate math.

The only book I really needed was my book *Masterpieces of Art*. It was lying in its usual spot under my pillow. I couldn't get it dirty because it had all my very favorite artists in it and told all about their famous lives and deaths. Mostly I like looking at the pictures more than reading all those little words, but I'm pretty sure I understand everything. I checked out *Masterpieces* from the Grover Cleveland library in kindergarten, but I like it so much that I'm never going to give it back. The school has sent about fifty late notices, but I don't care. I almost always get to the mailbox before Aunt Sylvia.

I also definitely needed my red artist suitcase, which was in its usual spot next to my bed. My suitcase used to be my mom's. Inside were some markers, a sketch pad, big paintbrushes and little paintbrushes, and tubes of paint in all sorts of colors. My mom left the red suitcase just for me. Because she had been a brilliant artist, too. And she would've been very, very famous if she hadn't died when I was only in kindergarten. That's how I know that artists usually die very young.

I stuffed my book inside my artist suitcase, snapped my suitcase shut, and stepped out into my new purple world.

Uncle Ralph was standing in front of the hallway mirror. Again. He was getting ready for work and already had his mail uniform on. He was combing out his orange mustache, which moved up and down every time he let out one of his loud chuckles. Today there was an extra-large cowboy hat on top of his head.

Uncle Ralph has a real job as a mailman. But someday he's going to be a very famous actor. That is why, he tells Aunt Sylvia, he has to talk to himself in his free time and practice his characters in front of the hallway mirror. Today after his mail route he had a very important audition for a very important cowboy play.

He scrunched his face at the mirror and cooed like he had a nose cold:

Howwwwww-dy

Then, he hiccupped:
"*How-how-how-deeee.*"

"Howdy, Uncle Ralph," I said, standing next to him in front of the mirror.

"Well, good mornin', Li'l Sport!" He put his arm around me like he was lassoing a cow. "What d'ya think? Do I make a darn good cowboy?"

"Uh-huh."

"You'd believe I was a cowboy, wouldn't ya? I mean, if ya saw me on the big stage?"

"Sure," I said.

"How 'bout the voice? YEEEE-HA! Or YEE-HAAAA!?"

"Both of 'em sound okay, Uncle Ralph. Both of 'em sound pretty darn good."

Uncle Ralph

But Uncle Ralph wasn't sure. He practiced cowboy faces in the mirror and tilted his head one way and then the other.

I tilted my head too. My plain ol' brown hair was flying in a million knotty directions under my purple artist hat. Bed head. And I still had pillow marks on my face. Bed face. Perfect.

"Hmmm," said Uncle Ralph as he took off his cowboy hat and sat down in the middle of the hall.

"Hmmm," I said as I took off my artist hat. I touched the special art napkin pinned inside. I ran my pinky finger along my mom's wild purple lines and curves.

"Uncle Ralph? Did you know that my mom had a Purple Period in her artist career?" I thrust my hat in front of his face so he could carefully study my mom's work.

"Well, no, I didn't, L'il Sport." He squinted his eyes at the napkin. "Would ya look at that?"

"It's very brilliant, isn't it? A very brilliant napkin."

"It most certainly is."

"My mom was definitely a very brilliant—"

"*Breakfast!*" Aunt Sylvia hollered, which nearly made me jump out of my tennis shoes. I snatched my artist hat back from Uncle Ralph and carefully put it back on my head. Then I stepped over Uncle Ralph and walked to the kitchen so he could practice some more.

Aunt Sylvia set a plate for me at the table. Two pieces of dry brown toast. She believes in a nonfatty breakfast. "Eat, eat," she said, swishing around the

kitchen in her dental uniform. "And kids? Don't forget. Thirty chews per—"

"Per swallow. I remember," I mumbled between crummy chews. As I was thinking about cows chewing cardboard, Cousin Junior attacked.

"Mission five-four-seven-three-eight. Come in, agent. Come in," he squeaked into his invisible walkie-talkie. "Mission: capture gooney alien cousin! Full speed ahead!" He ran back and forth in his plaid cape.

Zap-zing-pow! he shrieked, tying me up with Aunt Sylvia's knitting yarn.

"Aunt—Sylvia—" I choked out.

"Now we must try very hard to have good table manners," Aunt Sylvia replied with her back turned as she jellied Junior's toast at the counter. Without jelly, Junior would have tantrums under the table and throw toast at Aunt Sylvia. "We should *always* chew with our mouths closed—"

"But—"

"And *never* talk with our mouths full!"

"I—knowwww, b-b-b-but—"

"No big buts or little buts," chirped Aunt Sylvia, which made Junior hoot and haw like crazy.

"You both can eat your breakfast like polite little people. Right?"

I grumbled and fought my way out of that lousy yarn. When Aunt Sylvia turned around,

Junior was already sitting at the table like a polite little person. Aunt Sylvia opened the fridge and took out the milk just like every other morning—milk is very healthy for a child's teeth, Aunt Sylvia always says—and I couldn't help but notice my brilliant art Scotch-taped to the refrigerator. My paintings were hanging, as usual, right next to Junior's so-called art. Basically a bunch of scribbles. You'd never see such a thing at a gallery in Paris or Rome. Both of our paintings were splattered with leftovers and Junior's foody fingerprints. Obviously my relatives would *never* understand a brilliant artist.

JUNIOR

Uncle Ralph sat down at the table and set his cowboy hat down too.

"Now," said Aunt Sylvia, "tonight for Family Time I was thinking we should go to the Sleepy Beauty Botanical Gardens. What about that, kids? Doesn't that sound fun?"

Junior, Uncle Ralph, and I all groaned.

Then we groaned again when Aunt Sylvia set bowls of healthy mush in front of us.

"It looks like throw-up," whined Junior. He dipped his chunky finger into his bowl.

Zing!

"Eat your—um—oatmeal, Junior," said Uncle Ralph in his best father voice. He ate a spoonful. It got stuck all over his teeth and his orange mustache, just like glue.

"Honey?" He put his spoon down and cleared his throat. "This is oatmeal, isn't it?"

Junior and I cracked up like crazy. Junior was just about to throw a handful of his goo right at me when Aunt Sylvia finally sat down in her chair with a clunk. Her big hair drooped over her eyes. She breathed deep breaths, which is what she always does when we've stressed her out and she's on the edge of a morning meltdown.

"Off to school," I said. Really, a brilliant artist is better off not eating breakfast anyway. I threw some scruffy napkins into my suitcase, along with my crusty toast and some bananas and peanut butter and a whole jar of jelly. Then I made a wild dash for the front door.

"*Noonie!*" Aunt Sylvia yelped as she ran after me with a towel for my face and a comb for my hair. "Aren't those the pants you wore yesterday?

And your teeth—"

I sighed.

I had nearly escaped.

As Aunt Sylvia combed out my knotty hair in the bathroom and I was spitting minty-fresh toothpaste down the drain, I had a very important thought.

Some things may not be much different in my Purple Period. Well, at least not at first. Not until they all realize that I am a brilliant artist trapped in a fourth-grade body. Then things will definitely have to change. Then my dad will come and rescue me.

chapter three

The Artist's Unnecessary Education

A brilliant art life does *not* include elementary school.

Everyone knows that.

In my Purple Period I had way more important things to do. I was going to sip coffee from tiny cups and notice things that no one else noticed. I was going to have very serious conversations about art with lots of famous artists who all wore artist hats. And I was going to do my art. Of course. Every second that I wasn't staring at things or drinking coffee.

So I took my sweet time not going to school. I swung my suitcase as I walked, and I whistled, and I happened to notice all sorts of purple things. How strange that I'd never noticed them before! Unusually unusual. A purple ball, a purple slide, purple billboards, people wearing purple clothes. Purple purple purple.

Then I saw it: a tiny purple flower growing through a whole bunch of scraggly weeds. Perfect. The perfect purple landscape! Well, actually it was growing in a parking lot, but close enough.

Undoubtedly a sign.

Vincent van Gogh is one of my very favorite artists in my *Masterpieces* book. He painted all sorts of purple landscapes. And sunflowers and fields and faces. Once he ate his paints, which shows exactly how much he loved his art. Another time he cut off his ear and gave it to a lady as a present.

Afterward he painted a famous self-portrait with his ear missing. His short life is a very long story. If Vincent van Gogh were still alive, he'd understand me perfectly. Just like my mom would.

I snapped open my suitcase, took out a scruffy napkin, and began sketching.

"Get outta the parking lot, girly!" shouted a man in an orange car. He gave me a nasty glare and a honk. In fact, a whole line of cars started honking. But I just pulled my artist hat down over my ears and sketched mean eyebrows above my purple flower.

A woman in a van dug through her purse for parking lot money. "Poor thing," she clucked. Then she threw a quarter out her window, which landed right on top of my artist hat. I sketched quarters all around the eyebrows.

Down the sidewalk came an old man walking a fluffy dog on a purple leash. Perfect! Undoubtedly a sign. The perfect dog with a perfectly perfect purple leash.

I was just starting to sketch dog ears through the eyebrows and the flower and the quarters on my napkin when the cute dog broke free and ran like crazy straight toward me. I reached out to pet his little wet nose, and . . . that hairy dog

Honk!

lifted his leg and peed all over my tennis shoe. And my art!

My sketch ran in soggy doggy shades of purple yellow.

I couldn't remember reading about this sort of thing in my *Masterpieces* book.

I laid my napkin on the grass. Maybe a famous art dealer would find it and find me. That's all I really needed. Someone to discover me. And my art.

Just then a beat-up car drove by. It was put-putting so slowly that I could see a stack of white canvases filling the backseat and all sorts of other strange items: striped cloth, a large shopping mall mannequin, rusted lawn ornaments, baby-doll heads, and holiday lights all knotted up. The passenger side was crammed full with books and neon paints and plastic trolls and scissors.

I stood up. I waved my arms around. I jumped up and down and hollered, "Ms. Lilly! Hi, Ms. Lilly!" But she couldn't hear me. Her artist car was rumbling and shaking and blowing smoke like a volcano.

The only live person who understands me just perfectly is my art teacher, Ms. Lilly. My favorite teacher in the whole world. She teaches only Tuesdays through Thursdays, and on her free days, she told the fourth-graders, she does her art. Ms. Lilly is a real artist.

I had at least a hundred important questions to ask, but her artist car was already gone, headed for Grover Cleveland Elementary School.

When I finally escaped from school, I'd sure miss Ms. Lilly and art class. I sure would. But brilliant artists probably aren't even allowed to *have* art teachers. I sighed. I picked up my artist suitcase. Sitting in a parking lot can get a little boring. Besides, an artist needs peace and quiet.

Too late.

Hi NOONIE!

Reno was running toward me as fast as he could. Which was not very fast at all.

When Reno runs, his toes turn in and his knees turn out, and he's always carrying about a hundred enormous books. Reno is pretty darn short, but he's only in the third grade and might still grow. He falls flat on his face at least once a day. Today he didn't fall, but his books did. Right on top of my purple flower.

I sighed and sat back down. "Hi, Reno."

"I went—to your house, but you—were already gone!" Reno panted like crazy, pushing his old, dented glasses back up on his nose. His black hair was cut in jaggedy angles like a chipped china bowl. His shirt was buttoned straight to the tippy top of his neck. As always, his pants were wrinkle free—or they were until he'd been hanging out with me. Sometimes I thought that Reno was more like a hundred-year-old man than a third-grade boy. A total Math Person.

Reno and I are best friends. We walk to school together every day. Or at least we did in my Blue Period. My Purple Period was definitely a different life.

I crinkled up my soggy art napkin and threw it into my suitcase.

39

"Something smells funny, Noonie. And why are you sitting in a parking lot?"

A station wagon honked at us. I ignored it and put my nose high in the air. "Because an artist has more important things to do than going to Grover Cleveland."

"Like what?" Reno plunked himself down right next to me.

"Like looking at things and doing my art." I strummed my fingers on my *Masterpieces* book. "See, Reno, I'm going to be discovered any second now, and then I'll be famous."

"Wow," said Reno, fiddling with the calculator in his shirt pocket. "Is that why you're wearing that funny hat?"

I breathed a deep breath. Explaining art to the masses was getting very tiring. "It's an artist hat. My dad sent it all the way from China."

"Ohhhh." Reno nodded.

"My dad definitely understands my brilliant art now. He says that soon we'll be traveling all over the world to see my art in all sorts of famous galleries. Paris, Rome, China . . ."

"You're moving?" asked Reno.

"I'll have to. Soon I'll be way too big a fish for this little pond."

Reno looked all around the parking lot. "What pond?" He scrunched his face. "I thought your dad wanted you to stay here. Till you're done with school and everything."

"Oh, no. That's changed. Everything's changed, Reno. I just haven't had the chance to tell you."

"But we walked home together. Yesterday."

"I know, but all sorts of important things have happened since yesterday." I took off my artist hat and held it in front of Reno's face. "See?"

"An artist hat. I know."

"Yeah, but look inside."

"A napkin?"

"It's not just any ordinary napkin. My mom painted it."

Reno squinted his eyes, and he was going to touch my napkin, so I snatched my hat away and held it at a distance.

"It's pretty."

"I know it is. And did you happen to notice that it's purple?"

"Yeah, it's purple, but I don't get why you suddenly have to move because of a napkin."

I sighed. "Reno, this napkin is a *sign*, see. Because famous artists have different important periods in their artist careers: Blue Periods, Green Periods, Pointy Periods, periods with all sorts of cubes—so this obviously is the start of my very important Purple Period. And good things are going to happen. Like me getting discovered and traveling all over the place. I'm sure of it."

"I know, but you said you were gonna move at the beginning of first grade. And second grade, too. And—"

"No." I stuck my purple hat back on my head. "This time is very different. It's hard for you to understand, Reno. You can't possibly understand famous artists."

"Well, if you move—I mean, do you think I can visit you? In all those places?"

I shrugged. "I guess so."

"Maybe I can be your assistant. How 'bout that? Maybe I can even travel around with you sometimes."

"I'm not sure if famous artists can have assistants. I'm pretty sure that we have to work alone."

"But why?"

"That's just the way it is."

"Oh. Well maybe we can check in your *Masterpieces*

book." Reno pointed at my book, which I'd carefully laid on top of my artist suitcase. "Do you think there's anything about assistants in there?"

"I really doubt it." I flipped through the pages of my book, but I didn't have time to read all those little words. "Besides, it's not always an easy life traveling all over the place. I'll be riding on camels with my dad sometimes. And looking at wild yak bones. And I'll be very busy doing my art. Almost every second."

"That sounds okay. I mean, it sounds sort of fun. I'll look at bones too, and I'll help you be a famous artist."

I was just about to explain to Reno how doing art was not always fun. It was very serious work. I was just about to explain artistic temperament and the need for peace and quiet when we heard a familiar bicycle bell.

Rrrring-rrrring!

Sue Ann Pringle. Of course.

Definitely a sign. Sue Ann Pringle was pink, and I was purple. She was pretty curlicues, and I was dramatic lines and curves. Artistically opposite in every single way.

"Hi, Noonie! Hi, Reno!" She waved as if we were her best friends. Sue Ann was best friends with the whole world. She was riding her yellow bicycle with the banana seat; her pink handlebar streamers were flying behind.

"Hi, Sue Ann," we both mumbled.

"Aren't you two going to be late for school?" she hollered sweetly over her shoulder. Her banana curls, tied up in perfect pink bows, were flying too.

Sue Ann Pringle is the perfect fourth-grader. She always gets perfect grades, and she wins every single contest at school. She sells the most school candles and school calendars and school cookies every year, and she always wins the talent show for her perfect ballet routine. She stars in all the school plays, and always plays the part of a perfect girl who has a perfectly happy ending. No dog would ever have the guts to pee on Sue Ann Pringle. She's horribly perfect. Dogs can smell that a mile away.

So after Sue Ann was long gone on her lousy bicycle, I took out another napkin. I started drawing horribly pink bananas with my pink marker.

REPORT CARD
Sue Ann Pringle

Math	A
Science	A
Art	A
History	A
E.	A
	A
	A

perfect Sue ann

"Noonie?"

"Hmmm?"

"I'm not sure my mom will let me travel all over the place," said Reno. "I bet she won't."

"Yeah. Probably not."

"But then it'd be really sad if you did move away," said Reno, picking up a handful of grass and throwing it down again. "I'd have to walk to school by myself. And eat lunch by myself. I wouldn't really have anyone to hang out with. You know, at recess and after school and on Saturdays, when I normally hang out with you and we paint stuff, like when we painted your aunt's toilet seat and your uncle's mailbag. And who will I help

pringle

with homework? I like helping you with your math homework and all your other homework."

"You'd meet new friends, Reno."

Reno was quiet. He took off his glasses and wiped them clean with a tissue from his backpack. "I guess I could always ride my bike to school with Sue Ann. She lives right around the corner." He shrugged. "I guess she loves math."

I grumbled, "Yeah, she loves just about everything." I drew a pink bicycle being chased by a horribly hairy pink dog.

"I just—well, I don't know why you have to move away so fast to be an artist when there's an art contest right here."

I stopped drawing. "What art contest?"

"Ms. Lilly told all the classes about it last Thursday."

"Ms. Lilly?"

"At Grover Cleveland. I thought you knew about it."

I bit my tongue and racked my brain. How could I not have known about an *art contest*? Especially with *Ms. Lilly*! And that's when I realized that last Thursday I'd been sitting in Principal Baloney's office. Again. During art class. Because Mr. Weegel from social studies had sent me there for doodling in my social studies book. And for calling Principal Maloney a very original name: Principal Baloney.

"I mean it's not exactly like Paris or Rome or anything. It's just—"

I had already thrown my supplies back into my suitcase. I had already laid my *Masterpieces* book carefully on top of everything inside and snapped my suitcase shut. I was already running like crazy to Grover Cleveland Elementary School.

"Noonie! Wait!"

But I was way too excited to wait for Reno and all of his enormously boring books.

A contest. I could definitely win an art
contest. I *had* to win so my dad
would come flying home.
Pronto. Of course I'd
have to beat that
Sue Ann
Pringle,
but

in my **PURPLE PERIOD**
I could do just about anything.

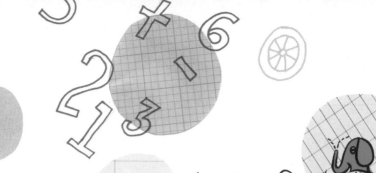

The Artist on Math and Elephants

"Noonie, you're late." Mrs. Tusk sighed and shook her bun head as I walked into math class smelling like a fire hydrant. "Again."

"Well, I know," I said. "It's just that . . ." I was going to tell Mrs. Tusk how I happened to drop my napkin sketch in a parking lot and a famous art collector happened to pick it up and was so amazed by my brilliant work that—

"No excuses, please and thank you," she snorted and gave me another mark in her big black book. Mrs. Tusk was used to my excuses. I had very artistic excuses every day. "Take out your math books, please!" she barked.

Mrs. Tusk was the sort of teacher you wondered about. What did Mrs. Tusk do after school? Did she make Mr. Tusk do addition and subtraction? Did she yell at him for being late? Did she yell at the grocery-store girl for charging the wrong price for cucumbers when they were supposed to be on sale?

Mrs. Tusk and I were opposites.

She was numbers, and I was pictures. She was Grover Cleveland and I was Paris, France.

"Today we're going to talk about . . ." Mrs. Tusk blabbed on and on with mathematical boringness.

My eyes grew heavy; my eyelids fluttered up and down. "Rounding numbers to the nearest hundred thousand . . ."

I was so bored that I had to doodle on my new math work sheet. I was thinking about the art contest. And my very brilliant masterpiece. Maybe I'd even paint Mrs. Tusk! With my award-winning art, I wouldn't even have to catch a new horrible exotic sickness. I would pack my artist suitcase and wave good-bye to Aunt Sylvia, Uncle Ralph, and Junior, and then my dad and I would fly off to just about everywhere.

"*Noonie?*" bellowed Mrs. Tusk. "I asked the class to open their math books. Did you not hear me ask the class to open their math books?"

I squeaked, "Uh—no?"

"And why is it that I don't even see a math book on your desk?"

"Well—uh—it's because I—uh—"

"No excuses, please and thank you." Mrs. Tusk tapped her chalk on her desk. *Tap-tap-tap.* "Do you have your math book, yes or no?"

"No. But—"

Mrs. Tusk's words were clogging my ears. I was practically deaf.

All the fourth-grade heads turned to look at me when Mrs. Tusk told me to go to the blackboard. I stared at my old grubby tennis shoes. One was stained yellow from the dog pee. Kids plugged their noses as I walked by. I heard Priscilla Peebody say, "*Pee-yoo!*" and Jimmy Jerkensdork said, "What's up with that funny hat?"

I stared at Mrs. Tusk's feet as she waited by her desk. Her pantyhose were clumped around her ankles, which made them look like tree trunks or wrinkled elephant legs.

Really, artists shouldn't have to mess with things as silly as large numbers. But I picked up the boring white chalk and scribbled Mrs. Tusk's math problem: 400,024 rounded off to . . .

I stayed at that blackboard for hours. Well, not really hours. Probably only a few minutes, but it felt like forever. I looked over my shoulder, and Sue Ann Pringle was wildly waving her hand around. She knew the answer. Of course she knew the answer. Sue Ann Pringle knew the answer to just about everything.

A drop of sweat dripped onto my nose. I blew hair out of my eyes. My purple artist hat suddenly felt like a flaming helmet.

"Ah-ha," said Mrs. Tusk like a clever spy. "Just as I thought, Noonie. Is there a *reason* you didn't do the homework for today?"

"Ummmm . . ." I had no idea what the answer was. I didn't even have any artistic excuses. I heard a few giggles, but I didn't

53

care because of course those fourth-graders couldn't possibly understand anything.

Mrs. Tusk sighed. "We just had a little talk about this before, Noonie. Remember? Yesterday." She scratched her bun.

Then, suddenly, I saw it. It was a broken piece of purple chalk at the very end of the blackboard. Definitely a sign!

So I grabbed that purple chalk and made a line going up, up, *up,* until I realized it was an elephant head. Brilliant. I drew the floppy elephant ears and the elephant body (very large) and a cute elephant tail curled up like a whirligig. I drew wrinkles at the bottom of the elephant's legs. I put a neat bun on top of my elephant's head. I got so involved drawing big husky tusks that I barely heard Mrs. Tusk saying, "*Noonie.* Noonie Norton!" I barely heard the class laughing out loud like wild yaks.

I didn't notice much of anything until Mrs. Tusk escorted me by the elbow with her mathematical fingers. She pointed and said, "To the—"

"To the hallway," I sighed. "I know."

I don't mind sitting in the hallway. I'm never sure what I'm supposed to be thinking about, exactly, but it's sure better than sitting in class. And teachers usually let me take my artist suitcase. They're afraid that if I'm bored, I'll bug kindergartners on their way to the bathroom.

I opened my suitcase and put my new purple chalk inside. Then I took out my *Masterpieces* book and turned to the chapter about Frida Kahlo.

Frida is one of my very favorite artists. Her mom first gave her some painting supplies when she was flat on her back, laid up in bed. Frida had been in a very scary trolley-car accident. Some artists love being in bed all day, but not Frida, because she got bored. She looked in her mirror and painted herself, over and over and over again. Self-portraits with Mexican monkeys and butterflies. Sad self-portraits with wounds and stitches.

I was just like Frida because *my mom* gave me painting supplies, too! Maybe I'd even do a self-portrait for the art contest. I'd win for sure. But it's very hard to paint yourself because you can never know exactly what you look like. In my Blue Period I

was blue; in my Purple Period I needed to be really purple.

I took my important supplies out of my artist suitcase, one by one.

There it was: a whole jar of grape jelly. Perfect. I carefully finger-painted my big round jelly head on the hallway floor. I bit a banana into little slices, which made perfect banana eyes. I made long lines of crunchy peanut-butter hair and slathered more jelly all over a triangle of toast. I carefully placed the perfectly purple toast on top of my jelly head. Of course my self-portrait wouldn't have been me without my artist hat.

As a final touch, I chewed the crust off another piece of brown toast. I gave myself a crusty frown mouth, just like Frida Kahlo's. Frida would have understood my brilliant self-portrait. Just like my mom would have. I was sure of it.

I looked up and saw Ms. Lilly coming down the hall. She was carrying about a hundred art supplies and was probably on her way to her classroom in the basement. I wanted her to see my brilliant art! I wanted to ask about the art contest! I was just about to shout "*Ms. Lilly!*" as loud as I could when suddenly large books were flying everywhere.

Reno. Of course. Slipping on my self-portrait. Reno is practically blind. His glasses, thicker than my jelly jar, flew out across the hallway floor.

"Noonie? Is that you?"

"Yes," I sighed, "it's me." My banana eyes were in my peanut-butter hair. My grape-jelly head looked like a perfectly purple monster. I glanced down the hall again and saw *Sue Ann Pringle* talking to Ms. Lilly. She just happened to be on her way out of the girls' bathroom, of course, and was probably asking Ms. Lilly a hundred questions so she could win the art contest.

"Can I sit here too?" asked Reno.

"Yeah, but I'm pretty sure that only artists and bad kids sit in the hallway, Reno. Math People never have to sit in the hallway."

Reno squinted his eyes and played with his fingers. "B-b-but," he stuttered, "but I'm not so busy. Can't I help you, Noonie?"

"Hmmmmmm."
I folded my arms

across my chest and tapped my triangle toast on my *Masterpieces* book. Reno didn't care. He plunked down next to me anyway. "Okay," I said, "you can be my assistant. For now." I put some banana chunks and a glob of peanut butter in his hand.

"Eww," said Reno.

At that exact second the school janitor came down the hall with his mop and bucket. He grumbled. And with one swish of the mop, my gooey purple face was gone.

chapter five

The Artist's Enormous Statement

GROVER CLEVELAND ELEMENTARY

I made a long line of carrots on the cafeteria table.

Aunt Sylvia's lunches were really very boring. Absolutely no color. No originality at all. Reno was eating the school lunch because he loved Chicken-Noodle-Soup Day. He slurped and slurped. For some strange reason he also loved carrot sticks, so I always very generously traded Aunt Sylvia's carrots for his chocolate chip cookies.

Sue Ann Pringle brought her lunch from home in a flowery lunch box. "Hi, Noonie. Hi, Reno," she said as she walked by our lunch table. She swung her lunch box back and forth.

"Hi, Sue Ann," we mumbled.

"Hey, are you two going to enter the school art contest?" Sue Ann asked, but we couldn't really answer because our mouths were full. Besides, I didn't want to give away any of my art secrets. Especially to *her*.

"I've been working on my painting every second," blabbed Sue Ann. "My mom says I should send it to a

magazine. Or an art gallery for kids. But I don't know. I still think it's just *horrible*." Sue Ann's mouth twisted up, and she wrinkled her forehead. I'd never seen Sue Ann worried about anything before.

She set her lunch box down on our table. She opened it with a snap. Reno and I both leaned over to see what she had for lunch. I gasped. Sue Ann Pringle's lunch box wasn't filled with lunch at all. It was filled with art supplies! Perfectly clean paintbrushes and little tubes of paint.

"My dad bought these for me at the art store," said Sue Ann. "I told him that I needed all the help I could get."

I set my cookie down. I cleared my throat and looked Sue Ann Pringle straight in the eye. "Well *my dad* says that my painting for the school art contest is the most brilliant work of art he's ever seen," I hissed. "And my dad's been all over the world. He can't wait for the art contest. He's absolutely positive that I'm going to win first prize."

Reno plunked down his soup spoon and gave me a look. "But—"

I stepped on his toe under the table. "*My dad* says that I'm probably going to be the next Vincent van Gogh." I put my nose in the air. "Or Frida Kahlo. A genius way, way ahead of my time." I very professionally snapped open my red suitcase. "And *my mom* gave me special art supplies."

Sue Ann Pringle looked inside. She crinkled her nose. "Well, your painting is definitely going to be the most original, Noonie."

She was terrified of me in my Purple Period. I was sure of it. She was used to winning everything. But of course Sue Ann Pringle pretended she wasn't a bit scared.

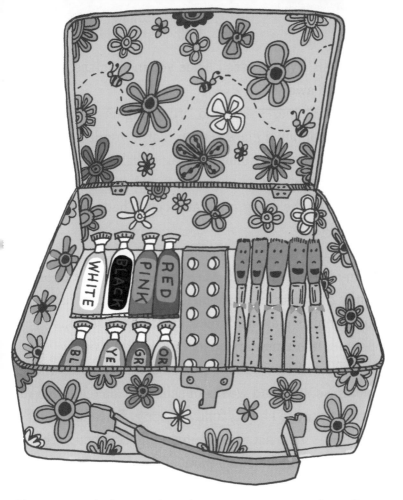

She just smiled sweetly in her annoying way. "I really can't wait to see it!"

"Me too." Reno shrugged. He slurped more soup.

Sue Ann snapped her lunch box shut, and I snapped my suitcase shut.

"Well, bye. I guess I'll see you in art class." She fluttered away.

"She's nice," said Reno, crunching on a cracker. And I shot him a glare scarier than a voodoo doll.

I'd have to do something big—really big and original—to beat that horrible Sue Ann Pringle.

Out on the playground at recess I had a big brilliant idea!

Andy Warhol and Jean-Michel Basquiat are two of my very favorite artists in my *Masterpieces* book. Andy's famous art is about soup cans, and bananas, and tennis shoes, and cows, and rows of famous people. In elementary school he caught a nasty disease, which made his skin all splotchy and made him miss days and weeks of school. Kids made fun of Andy because he was funny looking. Fortunately, his mom was an artist just like my mom! She bought him art supplies so he could paint and color and cut and paste all day in bed. Andy was a real artist. He didn't have to pay attention to those kids who didn't know anything. If Andy Warhol were in the fourth grade, we'd be best friends.

Andy was a great friend of Jean-Michel, who painted graffiti on subway cars and big buildings. He also made famous art with words and masks and stick people. He liked kids' art, so I was sure he'd have thought mine was absolutely brilliant.

Both of them made very important statements about their world. Just like I was going to make an important statement about my world at Grover Cleveland. It would be *so* big that my dad would certainly hear about it. All the way in China.

"He's funny looking." Reno squinted his eyes when I showed him the picture of the adult Andy Warhol, who was wearing a wig and enormous glasses. I told Reno that he got to pretend to be Andy Warhol because they both loved soup and they both wore funny glasses. "His art's kinda funny too," said Reno.

"Reno, it is *not* funny art. It is very important Pop Art." I tapped my purple chalk on my *Masterpieces* book.

"I love Pop-Tarts," said Reno. I sighed.

Of course, I got to be Jean-Michel Basquiat. My important job was to start our enormous art statement on the playground. I told

Reno that his important job was to dig through the cafeteria trash for anything that looked interesting. And artsy.

"Are we going to get in trouble?" Reno asked.

I stared at him. "You can never get in trouble for making *art*, Reno."

Reno shrugged and dashed off to his job. I took Mrs. Tusk's purple chalk and drew a line up one side of the playground, across, down the other side, and back again: an enormous square. I drew a big roof on top of the square, and big open doors, and a few crooked windows. A perfect purple chalk barn.

I wrote **V** on the barn.

I drew a chalky Principal Baloney and a wrinkled-elephanty Mrs. Tusk in the windows. Then I wrote all sorts of funny words all over the playground, like

POP-TART and **CHICKEN NOODLE** and **HORRIBLE** and **GRADE 4 FARM**. I darted in and out of hopscotchers and kickballers, jump ropers and four squarers.

Finally Reno came out of the cafeteria. His arms were completely full. So full that he kept dropping leftover sandwiches, half-eaten cupcakes, and fruit cups that rolled all over the place. He had to make three more trips because he'd also snagged about thirty dirty lunch bags, and best of all, he'd asked the lunch ladies for their extra-enormous chicken-noodle-soup cans.

"Excellent job, Andy," I said, and Reno beamed.

Reno cut eyes and mouths in the paper bags with scissors from his backpack. Meanwhile, I drew animal faces on all of them. Our own little art factory.

I told all the little kids to put the bags over their heads.

"Now," I hollered to the second-graders, "you're chickens, okay?"

The second-graders started to cluck as they stood in a jagged line and flapped their arms. "*Cluck-cluck-cluck,*" they screamed, just like they were supposed to.

The first-graders were cows and made *moo-moo-moo* sounds, and the kindergartners were my sheep, moaning, "*Baa-baa-baa.*" Some of the sheep and the cows started crawling around. The little kids definitely loved my art. All except Cousin Junior, who was hunting for plastic packages of cupcakes and Ho Hos.

I told Reno that we definitely needed animal tracks all over the playground. Not just fake tracks drawn with chalk, but real animal tracks. So I had all the little animals take off their shoes.

Reno had the important job of setting the shoes in place: under the swing sets, all over the grass, all around the barn, and up the steps of Grover Cleveland Elementary School. Brilliant.

The older kids didn't even notice us. At first. They were watching Sue Ann Pringle do perfect cartwheels in the grass. Her banana curls flew up and down. The kids would clap, and Sue Ann would say, "Oh, thank you." Her face would turn pink. "Thanks a lot. It's nothing, really."

But my art was getting very noisy. The older kids definitely noticed, and of course they wanted to be part of my art, too. My important statement was way more interesting than Sue Ann Pringle.

The fourth-graders got to hold the enormous soup cans and pretend to be the cafeteria ladies. The fifth-graders got to holler about rounding off horribly large numbers to the kindergarten sheep, who *baaed* even louder. The first-grade cows just played ring-around-the-rosy all over the place.

Soon you couldn't tell who was supposed to be what or what exactly was supposed to be happening. My chalk barn got all smeared, and animals with bag heads kept knocking into one another, and all sorts of toes got stepped on. I gave Reno the difficult artistic job of trying to herd the animals back into the Grover Cleveland barn.

Teachers looked out their windows and opened their mouths. The cafeteria ladies came outside and scratched their hairnets. I'm not sure if anyone really understood my brilliant work, but that's how the masses are.

I knew that Ms. Lilly understood it. I saw her look out her tiny basement window. She put her hand over her mouth, and I could've sworn she was laughing. I hoped that Ms. Lilly knew it was *me* who had created this unusually unusual masterpiece!

Sue Ann Pringle knew it was me. She walked straight up to me and laughed. "You're so funny, Noonie."

Hmmph.

Just then the bell shrieked. Recess was over, and so was my art. It was a stampede of little animals searching for their shoes. Reno got knocked over. And me? There was really no time to run and hide, the way real graffiti artists would. Reno and I were left standing all alone in the middle of our important artistic statement.

tick-tick
tic

chapter
six

The Artist's Body Art

I usually don't mind going to Principal Baloney's office.

There's always a blue bowl of sugar-free candy on a little table covered with smiling-kid magazines. I took a big handful of candy and threw it into my artist suitcase. But on this first day of my Purple Period,

I definitely didn't want to sit in Principal Baloney's office. I was missing art class. I watched the hands on the clock.

tick-tick-tick

I was so horribly bored that I took my purple marker from my jeans pocket and started to draw. First on my hand—the school secretary couldn't see that. And then I drew up my arm and all over the front of my jeans. Stars and flowers and weeds and trees.

Maybe I'd do brilliant body art for the school art contest!

I waited for Principal Baloney while he had a meeting with a mom and dad. As they left the office, they looked down at my purple jeans and my purple arm. Their kid probably wasn't nearly as bad as me. Then I had to wait as Principal Baloney talked to a curly-haired kindergartner. That kid came out crying, but I think it was only because he'd wet his pants. Principal Baloney made him go straight to the boys' bathroom. As the kindergartner ran out of the office, Sue Ann Pringle walked in.

Just my luck. Sue Ann had to pick up her trophy for perfect attendance.

"Hi, Sue Ann!" said the secretary with a huge smile. Sue Ann was best friends with every single adult.

"Hi!" Sue Ann looked down at me. "Noonie, you're in the principal's office? Again?" I fidgeted and tried to ignore her. I picked up a smiling-kid magazine and pretended to read. "Well, that was quite a *mess* you made out there on the playground. That poor, poor janitor." Sue Ann made a *tsk-tsk* sound as she shook her head.

"That was not a mess, Sue Ann Pringle," I hissed. "That was *art*." I stuck my nose high up in the air. Sue Ann simply giggled and kept giggling until I wanted to pull on her banana curls. She flashed her sparkly white teeth as she left the principal's office waving around her sparkly trophy.

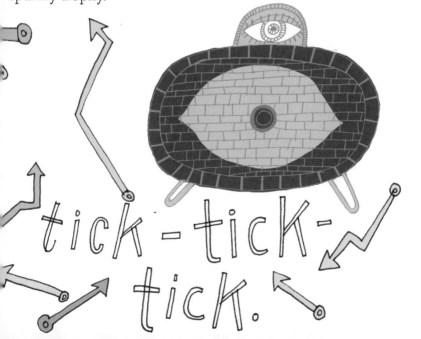

tick-tick-tick.

Ms. Lilly's art class was already half over. I couldn't miss her class. I had to hear about the art contest before it was too late!

"Well, Miss Norton," said Principal Baloney when I finally got to go in for our little talk, "it looks like you've gotten yourself into a bit of trouble. *More* trouble, that is. That's what it looks like to me." He sat back in his tall chair and fiddled with a pencil. He picked up a folder on his desk and put it down again.

"NORTON, NOONIE."

It was an awfully big folder.

"First, there was the vandalism in the hallway. Then the graffiti on the playground—"

"*Art*, Principal Maloney," I corrected him. "That was art."

Principal Baloney clearly didn't care about art. "Not doing your homework. Grades really not very good. Not even satisfactory."

I ran my finger up and down my brilliant art arm.

"And now you've colored all over yourself. Just like the kindergartners."

"Some women in Africa tattoo themselves. So do lots of artists all over the world. Body art is *very* popular these days."

Principal Baloney looked flustered. "We are *not* talking about . . . Africa. We are talking about *you*. Here. And either way, tattoos, or—or . . . this body art . . . is not acceptable at Grover Cleveland Elementary School."

My feet started to twitch, and my purple arm started to itch.

Principal Baloney made a coughing-choking sound. He picked up the "NORTON, NOONIE" file and leafed through the pages. "Hmmm." He tapped his thumb against one page. "Hmmm, hmmm." *Tap-tap.* "It looks like I'll have to give your aunt and uncle another call."

"That's not necessary!" I practically shouted. "Not necessary at all!"

"Really?" Principal Baloney folded his thick

79

hands on his desk. He pulled a yellow hanky out of his suit pocket and sneezed right into it. "Now why exactly, Noonie, is that not necessary?"

"Because my aunt and uncle are very, very busy people. My uncle is a famous actor, you know, and my aunt—well, she's very busy saving teeth. Besides, my dad says that he's going to pull me out of Grover Cleveland anyway. Probably tomorrow."

Principal Baloney raised his eyebrows, and I couldn't help but stare at his shiny, bald head under the office light.

"See, my dad says he's going to homeschool me. All over the world." I made a huge sweep with my purple arm. "We're starting with China. I'll learn calligraphy from all sorts of Chinese masters."

"China." Principal Baloney nodded.

"Mmm-hmmm. So you don't have to worry about me at all because I'm afraid you probably won't be seeing me. Ever again."

Once I was gone, Principal Baloney would miss me for sure. I think he was so choked up that he

80

didn't even know how to say good-bye. He puffed out his chest and rocked back and forth in his tall chair. "Noonie," he sighed, "do you remember when we had a little talk last week? And you told me that you were headed off to Malaysia with your dad to ride elephants and live in a hut?"

"Well, yeah. Malaysia didn't exactly work out. But China—"

"And before that you were moving to the Australian outback."

He obviously didn't understand anything, so I very professionally snapped open my suitcase. "Principal Maloney," I said as I leafed through my original paintings of my dad folded up in the back of my *Masterpieces* book. I held a painting up as evidence. "My dad *was* in the Australian outback. See?" My blue dad was riding on a blue kangaroo.

Principal Baloney squinted at my painting, then squinted at me.

"And that time he came home early because I had a terrible case of the Moldy Blue Fever? He wanted to take me with him to Australia for sure, but my aunt always says that his trips sound very, very dangerous. You never know what can happen out there in the outback. And before that? With those elephants? Well, I've really never liked elephants much anyway. But this time—"

"This time . . ." Principal Baloney tapped his sausage thumb on his sweaty forehead.

"I'm sure if you write him a letter—right this second—he'll be here pronto. And he'll take care of everything. I'll even help you write the letter if you want. I'll even put it in the mailbox."

I was starting to feel woozy. Probably another terrible case of some fatal fourth-grade sickness. But just then the bell rang. School was officially over for the day. I had missed all of art class.

"Uh—I have to go, Principal Baloney. I mean, Principal Maloney. I have a very important appointment. But it has been very nice getting to know you all these years. I've really enjoyed our little talks. And if you're ever in China—"

"Noonie—"

"I'm sorry, but I really have to go!"

I jumped out of the student chair so fast that Principal Baloney probably thought I had to go to the bathroom. I opened the big door, hurried past the secretary, dumped the rest of the blue bowl of sugar-free candy into my suitcase, and ran into the hallway. I heard Principal Baloney's voice echoing behind me like a spooky ghost: "Noonie! Noonie Norton!" But I kept running. Down two flights of stairs and straight to Ms. Lilly's art room in the basement.

The door was locked.

I sighed. I sat down with my back against Ms. Lilly's door.

The school janitor mopped the whole basement floor except the spot where I was sitting. "School is over," he said. "Time to go home."

Now I'd never find out about the contest. Now there'd be no blue-ribbon art that would bring my dad home.

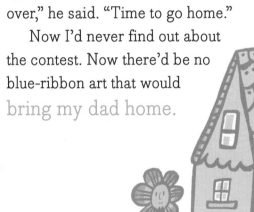

chapter seven
The Artist's Art Teacher

I
waited
outside
Grover Cleveland
for my dad to never come.

Reno had Math Club, so I had to walk to Aunt Sylvia and Uncle Ralph's house all by myself. I sat down on a patch of grass next to a gas station. I unwrapped four pieces of sugar-free candy and popped them all into my mouth.

I dug through my red suitcase and took out my purple marker and my new math work sheet. On the back of it I started my letter.

Dear Dad,

I hate to tell you, but I'm afraid that I've caught a terrible case of PURPLE PRINCIPAL PNEUMONIA. Undoubtedly from sitting in Principal Baloney's office. He sneezes like crazy and uses a hanky. You should probably come home PRONTO, before it's too late. . . .

I put my marker down—hmmm—and picked it up again.

But mostly I think you should come home to see my very famous art in the school art contest. Purple, just like mom's.

Love,
Noonie

I was just starting to draw myself surrounded by about twenty purple hankies when I heard a loud rumbling and a moaning toot of a horn. An old, beat-up car pulled over to the curb.

Ms. Lilly!

"Hi, Noonie!" she called out, rolling down the window of her passenger seat.

"Ohhhh, hiiii, Mmmm-Mmmm-Mssss. Lilly!" I garbled back with my sugar-free-candy mouth. "What luck," I thought. "How perfectly perfect. I couldn't find Ms. Lilly, but she has found me!"

"Do you need a lift home?" she asked, her face right next to a plastic troll.

"No. My dad is coming to get me. He should be here any second."

Ms. Lilly turned off her car and got out.

Her long artsy earrings dangled. Her short hair was sticking out in places, as if she hadn't even combed it. There were green streaks in her hair and an earring in her nose. She straightened the wrinkles in her exotic skirt. It must've come from somewhere far away, somewhere I'm sure my dad has been. Ms. Lilly smiled at me as she sat down on the curb. "We missed you in class today."

Ms. Lilly

"You did?" I wanted to tell Ms. Lilly that I *love* art class, I live for Tuesday through Thursday, and her class is probably the only reason I haven't already died a tragic death. Instead I blurted out, "I did a blackboard picture in math class, and then I did a self-portrait in the hallway, and then there was that playground Pop Art, and then I had to go to Principal Maloney's office."

"Again?" Ms. Lilly raised her eyebrows. She knew all about artists, how they're not skilled at school.

"Uh-huh. But my dad thinks I shouldn't waste my time on school anymore. Or math. He says I have more important things—"

"More important than school?" She ran her hand through her green streaks and looked straight at me.

"That's what he thinks." I shrugged.

Then I pretended to study Vincent van Gogh's very famous self-portrait in my *Masterpieces* book. It was the one where he had a bandage on his missing ear after he'd given the ear to that lady for a present.

"Well, I hope your dad knows that you have quite a talent for painting." Ms. Lilly smiled.

"I do?" I could barely contain my excitement! No real live artist had ever told me that before. But then I paused. "Oh." I said. "My dad knows that."

She looked down at my book and nodded to herself. "Van Gogh is one of my favorite painters."

"Mine too. But it's too, too bad that he died when he was so young."

Ms. Lilly nodded, and I was sure that I sounded just like a real Art Person.

Ms. Lilly said that even though he died awfully young, Vincent van Gogh painted a whole lot of paintings in his short life. I flipped through more pages of my book, and Ms. Lilly pointed out other paintings that she liked. I could hardly believe it. Ms. Lilly and I liked a lot of the very same artists. We both had excellent taste.

Ms. Lilly said that sometimes she liked to look at her favorite paintings for inspiration; sometimes she liked to read about the famous artists' lives, just like I did.

"Oh, by the way, nice arm," she said.

I looked down at my purple-marker arm. I'd forgotten all about it. "Thanks. It's not paint; it's just permanent marker."

90

Ms. Lilly laughed again. "Hmmm. I'm not so sure your mom will like it, then."

"My mom, she—" I suddenly felt a big fat lump in my throat. I touched my arm. "Oh, she won't mind. My mom likes all my work." And then I changed the subject. Pronto. "Um—Ms. Lilly? I wanted to ask you about the contest."

"The contest?"

"At school. The art contest."

"Oh!" Ms. Lilly put her hand to her head. "Right. I knew there was something I wanted to tell you. Well, the contest this year is about family. We want students to paint their families."

I choked on a sugar-free candy and felt it sink like a fish to the bottom of my stomach. I spit the other three onto the grass.

Ms. Lilly patted my back. "Are you okay?"

"I think so," I coughed out. "But, the contest—you mean, I have to paint a family?"

"Not just any family. *Your* family, Noonie."

Silence.

Ms. Lilly looked straight into my eyes again, with her artistic nose all crinkled up. "Is something wrong?"

"No. No, there's nothing wrong." I pictured my dad

fiddling with chopsticks and yak bones.

"But you'll have to hurry. The deadline is Thursday."

"Thursday?" I gasped. "*Two days?*"

Ms. Lilly nodded, and I said, "Well— um—I . . . well . . . sure. Yeah. I definitely can do that, Ms. Lilly. Definitely no big deal."

"Great." Ms. Lilly put her hand on top of my head, on my purple artist hat. "I hope your dad comes soon."

"Oh, he will," I lied.

Ms. Lilly smiled as she got up to go. She twirled her car keys on her finger.

"Um—Ms. Lilly?"

"Yes, Noonie?"

"I'm just wondering—well, do you think there are any *happy* artists?"

Ms. Lilly laughed, but it was a nice laugh. "Of course. Why would you ask that?"

I shrugged. "No reason." But I was secretly thinking about the famous artist Frida Kahlo painting herself with a frown mouth over and over in her bed. I was thinking about Vincent van Gogh with his crazy missing ear and his wild dotty paintings. I was thinking about Andy Warhol's funny wig falling into the trash as he hunted for soup cans and about Jean-Michel Basquiat and those graffiti artists running away from janitors and principals.

"A lot of artists I know are *very* happy. Of course sometimes they're sad too, but that's life, right?" Ms. Lilly dusted grass off her skirt. "That's what makes the world an interesting place." She gave me a sly smile and started walking to her car. Then she turned around. "And I just like to believe, Noonie," she said as she picked up a baby-doll head from her front seat and threw it in the back, "that *artists* have the power to change the world." Ms. Lilly stepped into her brilliantly beat-up artist car.

"But—" I called out as she drove away. I had so many questions. What was it like to be a *real* artist? Do dogs pee on artists more often than on normal people? Do artists ever make it to high school? What did Ms. Lilly do with the trolls and the holiday lights and the baby-doll heads? And what exactly did she mean when she said that an artist could change the world?

The Artist on Teeth and Tacos

"Noonie!"

I made a fast escape straight past Aunt Sylvia, who was knitting on the striped sofa. She hollered after me, "How was school, sweetie?"

"School was perfectly perfect, Aunt Sylvia!"

Aunt Sylvia loved to have auntie-niece bonding every day after school. But today there was no time for bonding.

"No principal's office?" she called out. "No trouble in math? No kids being mean?"

"Nope, nope, and more nope!"

I snuck past Junior, who was standing on his head in his super-action cape making noisy video sounds: *eeeep, slurp, zoom, pow!* I tiptoed straight past Uncle Ralph, who was in front of the hallway mirror.

I ducked into my bedroom and shut the door.

I took my purple marker out of my jeans pocket and stared at the white paper hanging on my empty easel.

A family?

I drew
a tiny
purple
Noonie
Norton
in the
middle
of my
paper.

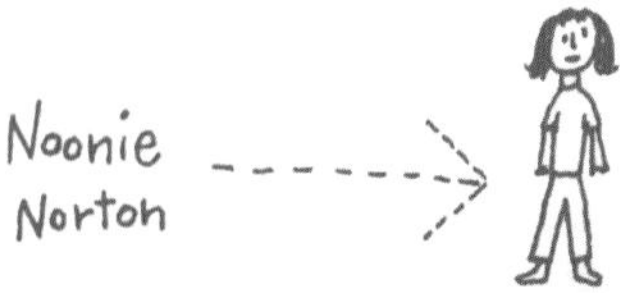

Noonie
Norton - - - - - ->

I tilted my head one way and then the other.

Artists don't need a family. Not really.

But Noonie Norton was awfully small. My paper looked like a big empty world, and I was tiny as a pea. It would never do. Never, never.

Then I had a brilliant idea!

I dug around for all of my old dolls under my bed. There were seven of them. I'd make a family, all right. There was a dad doll, sort of, and kind of a mom. The rest could be brothers and sisters. No cousins.

The artist doll family desperately needed artistic help. So I drew purple swirls all over their faces. I cut off their ears and strung dental floss through their heads. I gave them green paint streaks through their perfect hair and poked thumbtacks in their noses. Then I hung them all over me, as if they were twisted holiday lights and I were a tree. It was the coolest art family ever. For added effect, Aunt Sylvia's leftover knitting yarn went around my head, and one of her half-knitted socks dangled off my nose.

Maybe I could do performance art for the art contest! It would definitely be *very* original. My audience would be shocked and thrilled. They'd observe me for hours and take a whole bunch of notes.

I decided to test out my brilliant art on Uncle Ralph. So I inched myself into the middle of the hallway. Then I posed. Then I changed poses. I cleared my throat. I wanted to itch my toe, but I wasn't sure if art is allowed to move.

Uncle Ralph was very busy practicing for his next audition.

His costume looked like a small ship around his middle, with only his legs and his head sticking out. There were enormous pieces of fake lettuce and tomato and cheese toppings sprouting from his waist. "TAAAA-co" and

TAAA - COooo

he practiced in his best voices.

"You didn't get the cowboy part, Uncle Ralph?"

Uncle Ralph shook his head. "Not that one, Li'l Sport. But the show must go on. That's what they say."

"Now you want to be a . . . taco?"

"It's a very important weekend role for that new restaurant, Mr. Taco. It's the starring role. What about you, Li'l Sport? What part are you auditioning for? I've never seen that kinda costume before."

"I'm trying to win the art contest at school. It's not a part, exactly. I'm performance art."

Uncle Ralph scratched his head. "Hmmm. Performance art. Is there a script for that sort of thing?"

"I don't think so. I'm pretty sure I'm just supposed to stand against the wall with the other paintings."

"Difficult. Very difficult. I suppose you'll have to express yourself with your face alone. And gestures, Li'l Sport. All kinds of gestures." Uncle Ralph practiced dramatic gestures in front of the hallway mirror. He raised his arm in the air and wiggled his hips. He made all sorts of faces: sad, happy, mysterious, scared, shocked, and amazed. I practiced my faces, too. I bounced up and down and made the dolls' heads shake.

Uncle Ralph shrugged, and I shrugged too.

"Hmmm," he said.

"Hmmm," I agreed.

Uncle Ralph sat down, and I sat down next to him. He put his arm around my shoulder, on top of the dad doll's head.

"Now, take it from me, Sport: The arts biz is dog-eat-dog. There are always 'bout a hundred artists just around the corner waiting to be discovered." Uncle

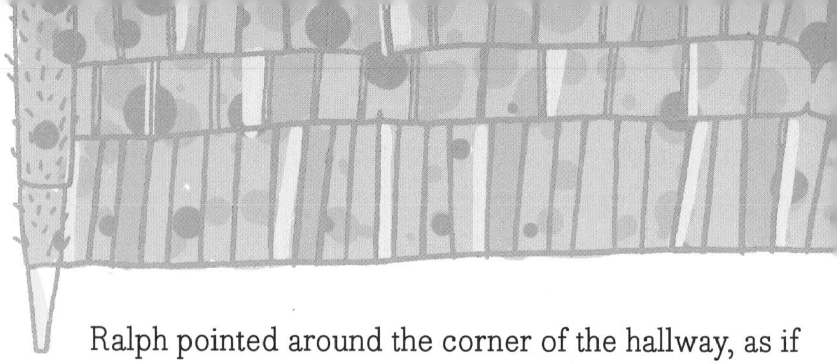

Ralph pointed around the corner of the hallway, as if artists were lurking there. I imagined a hundred Sue Ann Pringles. "And the critics like to chew everything apart."

"They do?"

"Most definitely. Trust me, Li'l Sport, you're much better off thinking practical."

"Practical?"

"Have you ever considered being an accountant?" he asked, and I shook my head. "A firefighter? Or an astronaut? Maybe you should consider being a zookeeper or a hairdresser. How 'bout a game show hostess? Car dealer? Mail carrier?"

"But my teacher Ms. Lilly says that I have quite a talent for art."

"Talent? I know you do, Sport. Just like your mom. But look at me. All the talent in the world and still not a star." He itched his corn shell and hiked up his cheese topping. "I'm a talented taco."

Uncle Ralph had a point. But even though he understood about acting—maybe he'd even get discovered someday soon—I didn't think he understood much about famous artists.

I helped Uncle Ralph practice being a taco with his taco script until I got tired of playing the burrito. I didn't like hollering about beans and tomatoes. I still thought that it sounded much better to be a famous artist, even if it wasn't practical.

I scooted myself into the living room. Right in front of the TV.

Aunt Sylvia was watching her favorite soap opera. She leaned to one side of

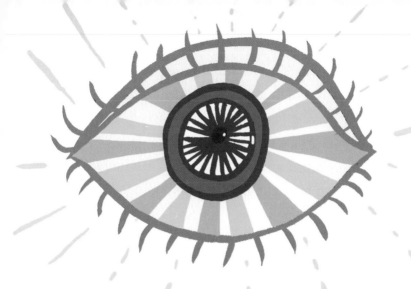

the striped sofa so I wouldn't block her view.

"Aunt Sylvia, guess what? My art teacher says I'll probably be a famous artist someday. She says I have *quite* a talent."

Aunt Sylvia's TV eyes were huge. "That's great, sweetie! A famous artist?"

I shrugged. "That's what she says."

"Oop. Hold on a sec, Noonie. This is the really good part."

Aunt Sylvia loved the striped sofa and her soap operas. Sometimes I wondered what would happen if scary bearded burglars broke in and stole the sofa. Aunt Sylvia would probably be stolen too.

"Don't do it, Monika!" Aunt Sylvia gasped at the TV. Her eyes were practically popping out until she covered them with her hand. "Don't go in there. *No!*"

I sat down next to her. It was definitely the good part.

Boy, did those soap opera people have some horrible times. They hated each other one second and loved each other the next. You just never knew what was going to happen to them.

Maybe I could paint a fake soap opera family! The masses loved soap operas. I'd probably win for sure. But I decided that the fake family was just a bit too fake. Brothers drowned, sisters caught on fire, mothers were poisoned, fathers mysteriously disappeared, and all of them had terrible diseases. The judges at the art contest would never believe me. No family had *that* much love and death.

"Sweetie?" Aunt Sylvia suddenly took her eyes off the TV and turned to me. "Why are you wearing those funny baby dolls? And why is my half-knitted sock on your nose?"

"I'm art," I said with a dramatic gesture.

"Art?" She crinkled her forehead and sat up even straighter on the sofa. She unraveled the yarn and took the sock off my nose. "Who's Art?"

I sighed and stood up from the striped sofa. That's when Aunt Sylvia turned off the TV and announced that it was Family Time. "Honey?" she called to Uncle Ralph. "Honey? Don't you want to go to the Sleepy Beauty Gardens? I've been talking about going there forever!"

Uncle Ralph hollered a bit louder about tacos and tomatoes.

"Well—or maybe we could play board games after dinner? How 'bout that, Noonie?"

I struck an artistic pose and made a face expressing horrible shock.

"Or—well, maybe we could all just watch a movie together. Maybe eat some popcorn? Doesn't that sound fun?"

Cousin Junior raced through the living room yelling something about superpowers as his green cape flew behind him. Superpowers? I *definitely* could use some superpowers. Superpowers would get me out of Family Time. And maybe with super artist powers I could change my world, just like Ms. Lilly had said. So for the first time in my whole life I ran after Junior and begged him to capture me.

"Really?" he asked. "You want to play with *me*?"

Junior tugged me along by a baby-doll leg and led me out to his "headquarters"—basically a tree stump in the middle of the yard. "You're definitely the best alien I've ever caught," he said.

"I'm not an alien. I'm an artist."

"Same thing." He plunked me down on the stump and sat next to me. We swung our legs back and forth. We listened to the neighbor's wiener dog howl, and we giggled at a teenager kissing her boyfriend in his car.

Finally Junior pulled a slew of cookies and chocolate bars from under his green cape. He crunched into a cookie. Then he unwrapped a candy bar and practically ate it whole. "You have to starve, alien artist prisoner!" he growled at me with chocolate teeth.

I just shrugged. "That's okay. Artists always starve. See, no one buys our paintings, and critics chew everything apart."

Junior yawned and bit into another bar. "Fine, then." He threw a chocolate bar, and it landed in my lap. "I'll buy one of your alien paintings—for one chocolate bar. But it's your *last* meal."

It had to be performance art, of course, because I was taken prisoner without my art supplies.

Junior giggled as I smudged chocolate curlicues all over his arms. And nougat on his neck. And marshmallow on his mouth. "*Pow, rrruff, slurrrp, gooey,*" he said. I finger-painted "Planet Weirdo" in chocolate on Junior's green cape. When I was painting nuts on his nose, he laughed so hard that I thought he might wet his pants, which he does sometimes.

"Are you having fun playing with me, Noonie?

It's fun, isn't it? I might give you more candy tomorrow if you—"

Unfortunately, the candy turned out to be a little problem. Junior's stomach lurched. He heaved and hoed. And suddenly . . . Junior lost his cookies and threw up all over the place.

"Sick," I said.

"*Mom! Mommy! Mom!*" blubbered sick Cousin Junior. He flung himself away from the stumpy head-quarters and back into the house like a superhero.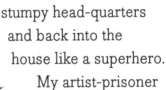

My artist-prisoner life was over. I was free.

I slunk back to my bedroom. I took off my baby-doll family and tossed them under my bed. Then I closed my eyes and counted to thirty. "I believe that artists have the power to change the world," I said to my painting. "Artists have the power to change the world. Artists have—" I wished

Ms. Lilly were here. Did artists have the power to make the world better? Or just plain ol' crazier? I wasn't sure I understood much of anything. If artists had some sort of superpower to change the world, why didn't I even have enough artist power to make my dad come home? Pronto?

"*Zap, zing, poof!*" I hollered. I turned some fast twirls and waved my arms. "Abracadabra! Abracadabra!" I jumped up and down on my bed. "Famous artist Noonie Norton demands that her dad come home *right this second!*" I opened one eye. "*Pronto?*" I opened the other eye.

Nothing.

So I stomped off my bed and threw a handful of purple paint at my paper.

Jackson Pollock is one of my very favorite artists in my *Masterpieces* book. Mostly I like him because he brilliantly flung paint at a lot of blank canvases on his floor. He dripped and splattered and poured and hurled paint. And he didn't use regular old brushes. Oh, no. He used knives and sticks and other interesting things as he moved—like a crazy dancer with superpowers—all around his paintings.

Which is exactly what I did. I took my painting off my easel and laid it on the floor. I danced around a little. Then . . . *drip, drip, splat, splat, purple, purple.*

You couldn't see tiny Noonie Norton anymore. I was positive that Jackson Pollock would have loved my splattery painting. I wanted him to step right out of my *Masterpieces* book and throw paint with me. It was very brilliant art, of course, even if it definitely wasn't a family painting.

I crinkled up my drippy painting into a tiny little ball and threw it under my bed next to my dirty clothes and my math book.

Poor me. Poor Noonie Norton. I had a terrible case of artist's block. And no real family to paint.

chapter nine

The Artist's Hidden Purple Presents

The second day of my Purple Period went like this:

Rrrrrrrring! Seven o'clock.

I pulled my purple artist hat over my face and snorted.

And then I felt my mom's napkin painting. Right against my nose. I immediately threw off my pillow and then my covers. Even though artists are supposed

to sleep all day, I got out of bed and walked straight to my closet. I dug through my piles of clothes as if I were doing an important archaeological dig.

In the very back of my closet I found my special cardboard box. I pulled it out carefully as if it were an ancient bone or a mummy's pot of gold.

My dad had given me the important job of keeping the cardboard box safe. He'd taken a few things to remember, but fortunately he hadn't taken most of them, because they would've gotten dirty for sure. He might've lost them on a sheep farm in New Zealand or on a wild safari in Kenya.

I opened the lid and took a handful of pictures and laid them out on my floor. Pictures of my mom and dad when they were still sort of young. There were pictures of me as a fat drooling baby and pictures of my mom smiling and pictures of my dad digging for weird things. There were some paintings in the box, too. My mom definitely had had a Blue Period, but hers was much prettier than mine. Hers was more like a Sky Blue, not a stormy Black and Blue. Her head was never squiggly, and her mouth was never a jagged blue frown. But I couldn't find any of her purple paintings. Hmmph. None at all.

I reached my hand down to the very bottom of the box. And then I found it! It was my favorite picture of the three of us, with me in the center of everything. Even better, my mom was wearing a purple dress! Definitely a sign.

"Hi, Noonie!"

I almost jumped straight out of my artist hat.

"I came early today so I wouldn't miss you."

That Reno. I quickly stuffed everything back in my box, everything except for my favorite family picture. I crammed the lid back on and shoved it back into my closet and covered it up with wrinkled clothes. "I'm afraid that I have no time for school, Reno," I told him. "I have to work on my painting for the art contest. All day."

He looked at my empty easel. "No offense, but I'm just wondering—I mean, if you're going to be a famous artist, then how come your painting's all white?"

I shot my best soap-opera-star glare at him. I took my purple paint and my biggest brush and suddenly, with artistic flair, painted purple streaks all over my paper. "There. Now it's not just white paper anymore, see? It's the beginning of a masterpiece!"

"Ohhhh," said Reno, squinting his eyes. "But, Noonie? Um—as your assistant, I think that maybe you should at least go to art class today. Maybe Ms. Lilly can help you. I bet she can."

Hmmm. Reno had a point, even though I was pretty sure that assistants weren't supposed to give advice to their famous artists.

"I bet that Sue Ann Pringle is getting all sorts of help from Ms. Lilly on her painting," added Reno. "She probably asks Ms. Lilly all sorts of questions."

Sue Ann Pringle? That's when I stuck the picture of my family into the back of my *Masterpieces* book and snapped my artist suitcase shut. I pulled Reno behind me as I made a wild dash for the front door.

Unfortunately, Aunt Sylvia spotted us and made us sit down for breakfast. Raisin bran with something sprinkled on top and some sort of health muffin that was heavy as a rock. While Aunt Sylvia had her back turned, Cousin Junior threw his muffin to Uncle Ralph like a football, and I threw mine into my artist suitcase. Reno politely ate the whole thing even though he'd already eaten breakfast.

"Off to school!" I said, leaping out of my chair.

"Noonie? Wait a sec, sweetie!"

I sighed. More face cleaning and hair brushing and teeth flossing.

"There's a special present for you under your bowl," said Aunt Sylvia.

A present? I sat back down.

There was a hush around the kitchen table. Uncle Ralph and Aunt Sylvia and Cousin Junior and Reno all leaned over as I lifted up my cereal bowl.

My mouth opened wide, and my heart practically flew out of my chest. I could hardly believe it! There was a little stack of purple postcards. But they weren't just any ordinary postcards. Oh, no. They were postcards that my mom had painted herself. A long, long time ago. How perfectly perfect. I hadn't been able to find my mom's brilliant purple work, but it had found me.

"Your mom wanted to be a famous artist, too." Aunt Sylvia smiled at me. "I dug those postcards out of the attic, sweetie. I think she had quite a talent for painting, just like you." She tilted her head. "And I guess your mom must've really liked purple."

"I know. Her Purple Period," I practically whispered. I had to swallow the lump in my throat, which was worse than swallowing Aunt Sylvia's muffin.

I didn't even mind brushing my teeth then or letting Aunt Sylvia comb out my knotty hair. I didn't mind having Aunt Sylvia wash my face, and I didn't mind washing my hands with soap in the sink.

On the walk to school I looked at the postcards over and over. "Dear Sis," they all started, and they all ended with "Wish you were here!" They all had very interesting stamps from funny foreign countries: the Philippines and Pakistan. India and Iceland. Brunei and Barbados. My mom's Purple Period must've been her traveling period. With my dad. All over the world.

"May I see?" asked Reno.

Dear Sis,
I've ...
...
... wish you were
here! love,
Syl.

Sylvia ...

Unfortunately, as I held the postcards out carefully in my hand, Reno tripped on the sidewalk, his glasses flew off, and he landed straight on his calculator. Again.

Reno desperately needed artistic help. Usually I'd draw a new pair of permanent-marker glasses on his face, but today I was way too excited to get to Grover Cleveland Elementary School.

"Noonie! Wait!" called Reno, running after me in his lopsided way and dropping his books.

I guess the life of a Math Person can sometimes be difficult too.

chapter ten

The ARTIST'S BLOCK

was a perfectly perfect student all day. I was probably even better than Sue Ann Pringle. I didn't get
sent to the hallway, and I didn't have to go to Principal
Baloney's office. I didn't draw elephant pictures of
Mrs. Tusk or brilliant scowl-face self-portraits like
Frida Kahlo. I definitely didn't cause any artistic
trouble on the playground. I couldn't miss art class.

And finally it was time.

I was the very first fourth-grader in Ms. Lilly's
classroom. I even beat Sue Ann Pringle, who walked
in after me for once and, unfortunately, set up her
easel right next to mine. She organized her paints
like the colors of the rainbow and lined up her clean
brushes from biggest to smallest. She tied her pink

painter's smock around her waist and waited patiently for Ms. Lilly's important lesson.

Ms. Lilly tried to teach the fourth-graders about abstract art. "You don't have to paint what your family really looks like. Paint them how your artist mind *sees* them," she told us. A feeling, an impression, an abstraction. Ms. Lilly showed us a painting by Pablo Picasso as an example. Lots of freaky circles and squares that ended up looking like a person. Sort of.

Out of the corner of my eye I snuck a peek at Sue Ann Pringle.

She stepped back to study her painting. I wanted to study her painting, too, but I couldn't even get a good look. All I could see was Sue Ann's face. She scowled and frowned. Her forehead was crinkled as she sighed and blew blond hair out of her eyes. Then she picked up her paintbrush and dabbed it into her pink paint.

I suddenly felt a little sick. I was absolutely positive that I was coming down with a very deadly disease. Yes. It was undoubtedly a case of . . . *The Scream*!

Edvard Munch is one of my very favorite artists in my *Masterpieces* book. He painted a very famous painting called *The Scream*. Edvard liked to paint things from his life, but unfortunately he had a life where all sorts of terrible things happened to him. For one, his mom died when he was only five years old. If Edvard Munch and I had been in kindergarten together, we would've been best friends.

In Munch's painting, the screamy man's body is all googley, his eyes are bugged out, and his mouth is caught in a big screamy O. Very scary.

So I made a scream face at Sue Ann Pringle.

But she just giggled and said, "You're so funny, Noonie!"

I sighed. I turned my easel so Sue Ann definitely couldn't see my empty painting, and then I opened my *Masterpieces* book. I didn't look at famous paintings this time. I turned to the very last page and took out a stack of little folded paintings by *me*: paintings of my mom and dad on the back of math work sheets, on napkins, and on brown paper bags.

I squeezed my eyes shut. If only *my mom* would step straight out of my *Masterpieces* book.

"Brilliant art, Noonie. Bravo! *Magnifico!*" she'd say for sure.

And I'd say, "Brilliant purple postcards, Mom."

I opened my eyes and sniffled. I folded up all of my original art and carefully placed it in the back of my *Masterpieces* book. Someday I'd make *really* brilliant art. Like her. And my dad would fly home in about one second.

I stared at my big piece of purple paper hanging on the school easel.

And then I stared some more.

Nothing but empty purple.

I tilted my head one way and then the other.

I played with my paintbrushes and put them all in a straight line, just like Sue Ann's.

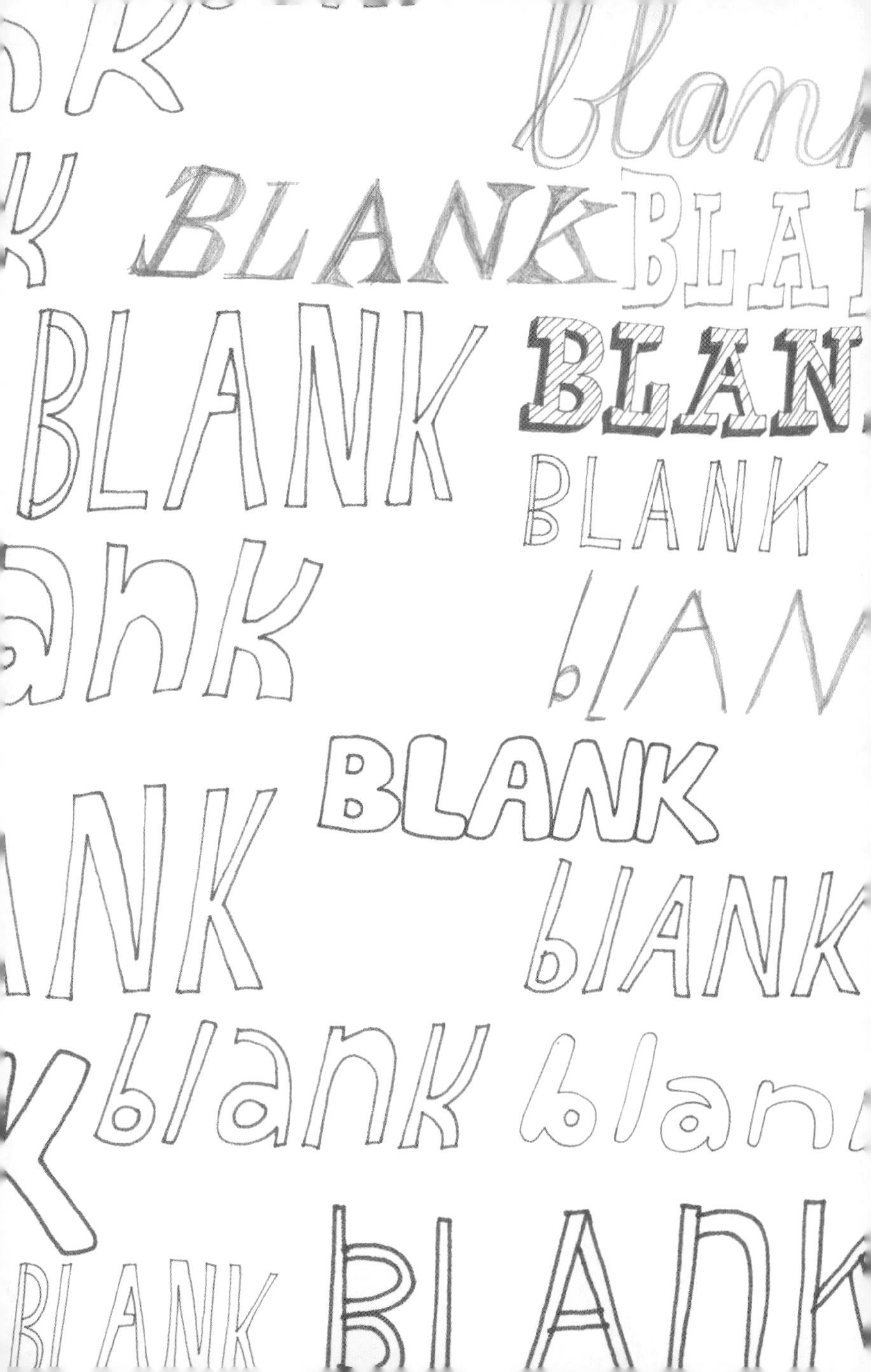
BLANK
BLANK
BLANK
BLANK
bLANK
blank
BLANK

I

was

waiting

for

some

sort

of

artist

power.

tick - tick -
tick

But I had been staring for a few hours, or at least a lot of minutes, and I still couldn't think of how to paint my family.

"How's it going, Noonie?" Ms. Lilly asked, stopping at my easel to take a serious look at my purple painting.

"Not so well, I guess," I mumbled out the side of my mouth. I couldn't let Sue Ann know that things weren't perfectly perfect. "Ms. Lilly, I was just wondering . . ." I squirmed and twitched and poked my finger in my purple paint. "Do you think an artist has ever died from artist's block?"

Ms. Lilly laughed. "I don't think so, Noonie. Sometimes I think that artist's block is a good thing."

I scrunched my face.

"I know it can feel pretty lousy. But maybe it means that you're trying to figure something out." Ms. Lilly smiled and put her hand on my purple artist hat. "Sometimes when I have artist's block, I find out that the answer—what I needed to paint—was actually right under my nose. It just took me awhile to see it."

"Really?" I scratched my head. "But when you have artist's block, do you ever wish that all your favorite artists could step right out of your *Masterpieces* book? I mean, so you could ask them things? And they could help you?"

Ms. Lilly thought hard about that one. She was quiet.

I hoped she wasn't thinking, "That Looney Noonie." But all of a sudden Ms. Lilly's face broke into a huge smile. "I'd love that, Noonie," she said. "I'd love to talk to my favorite artists. So they could help me. I'd have all sorts of questions."

"Me too!" I beamed. Ms. Lilly understood me perfectly.

Then the bell rang, and the happy fourth-graders left their art and ran out the door toward home and other happy things.

Ms. Lilly started cleaning everything up, scrubbing paint splotches off the floor. Her short hair was flying in a million directions, and there was paint streaked across her paint smock. Ms. Lilly was a real artist. But she took one look at me—the only one left in the whole classroom—and stopped scrubbing.

"Ms. Lilly?" I asked nervously. "How come everyone is painting such pretty things? What if I don't want to paint pretty things?"

She pulled up a chair and sat down right next to my easel. And then Ms. Lilly told me all about her art: the work she did with baby-doll heads and holiday lights and neon paints and mannequins. Wow! Ms. Lilly had quite an imagination.

"My art is probably a bit weird for most people, Noonie. Not exactly pretty. And I definitely don't win that many art contests. But I don't want to quit. Do you know why?"

I shook my head and asked very quietly, "Why?"

"Well, because when I'm painting, it's just me. And my art. I think I'm lucky—you and I are lucky—to feel so passionate about something. About our work. That's what counts, right? More than having other people like it. More than winning any old contest." Ms. Lilly ran her paint-splotched hand through her hair. Now she had green and red and yellow stripes. "We may paint things that make people uncomfortable, Noonie. We may paint things that we'd like to change in our world, and sometimes—well, that's not going to be pretty."

"Sure," I said. I picked up my red artist suitcase and took my purple painting off the easel. But I wasn't sure.

Not sure at all.

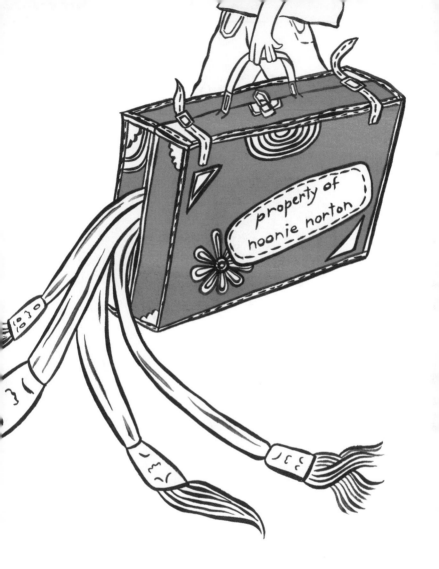

property of
hoonie norton

The Artist Finally Paints Something

While I was walking home to Aunt Sylvia and Uncle Ralph's house, I had a brilliant idea! My feet were filled with a bouncy artistic inspiration. I couldn't even stop to notice purple things. When I opened the mailbox and there was nothing for me, I didn't even feel sad.

"*Hut, hut . . . hike!*"

Uncle Ralph was throwing a ball to Junior, who was running back and forth across the yard. Junior's green superhero cape flew behind. "*Slurp! Yow! Zowwwy!*" he hollered as he missed every time.

Uncle Ralph threw the football to me, and I caught it on my first try, even with my purple painting under my arm. "*Touchdown!*" shouted Uncle Ralph, throwing his arms into the air. "Have you ever considered trying out for the football team, Li'l Sport? You really have quite a talent!"

That's when Aunt Sylvia came out onto the porch and called the three of us inside. In her hand was a letter with a funny-looking stained stamp. I dropped the football on my toes. Aunt Sylvia had gotten to the mailbox before me.

We filed into the family room, and she patted the striped sofa so we'd all sit down. I was smooshed like a hamburger patty between Aunt Sylvia and Uncle Ralph. Then Aunt Sylvia turned her soap opera off. This was very serious. "Sweetie," she started, tilting her head and looking straight into my eyes, "I got a letter from your dad today. Now for some strange reason he's afraid that you're very sick *again*."

"Sick?" I asked.

"Sick?" asked Uncle Ralph. "Oh, no! Are you sick, Li'l Sport?" He made me stick out my tongue so he could see if it was the right color. He peered

carrot
ice cre

into my ears looking for strange rashes or strange growths. Nothing. He was just about to examine my purple arm when I sat on my hand and tried to cover my brilliant body art with my artist hat.

"Um—well . . ." My terrible case of *The Scream* had mysteriously gone away; my artist's block was cured, and so were all my other fatal fourth-grade sicknesses. "See, I was sort of sick—yesterday—but now—well, I feel just fine." I was itching to paint my masterpiece. I scooted and squirmed on the striped sofa. "I feel pretty darn fantastic."

Aunt Sylvia gently put her hand to my cheek. Then she felt my forehead to see if I had some strange exotic fever. "Are you sure, sweetie?"

I nodded like crazy.

"You probably aren't getting enough fiber. Or green vegetables."

Ick. Green vegetables?

"And you definitely need more exercise."

Exercise? Definitely not.

broccoli
ice Cream

"Why don't we start having family exercise night!" carried on Aunt Sylvia. "How about that? Doesn't that sound fun?"

Junior and Uncle Ralph and I groaned. Uncle Ralph patted his big belly, and Junior itched his chunky chin.

"Ice cream might do the trick again, honey." Uncle Ralph scrunched his face.

Junior and I nodded.

"And my mom's purple postcards?" I added quickly. "Those did the trick, too."

"Oh." Aunt Sylvia's eyes brightened, and her cheeks turned pink. "Well—"

"I'm fine, Aunt Sylvia. I feel just great!" I leaped off the couch and did a few jumping jacks. "Really. Couldn't feel better. Perfectly perfect."

"Well, okay." Aunt Sylvia wiped her worried forehead. "But you've had an awful lot of serious mysterious sicknesses lately."

Silence.

Uncle Ralph cleared his throat. "Now, Li'l Sport," he said without any of his funny acting voices, "you and me and everybody else know that your dad would *love* to be here right this second. With you. Right?" Uncle

Ralph acted like he was talking to a packed audience. "Am I *right*?"

Aunt Sylvia was the only one nodding. "You know that he's so very busy. With his very important work."

"Very busy," agreed Uncle Ralph.

"But he certainly won't be gone forever," said Aunt Sylvia.

We'd had this little talk before. Busy, busy. Just how busy can a person be?

My mouth turned into a jagged frown.

Aunt Sylvia put her hand on my purple artist hat. Then she tried to carefully comb out my messy hair with her fingers. "Now, you know that your dad comes home after every single trip. And you also know that you're always part of our family. Forever."

"You sure are," said Uncle Ralph. "Just like an ant in our colony. A little bee in our beehive. A pea in our pod. An—"

"An alien in our pod, too," added Cousin Junior.

I stared at Aunt Sylvia and Uncle Ralph and Junior. I gulped.

It *was* right under my nose.

"Where are you going, sweetie? We're going to

have Family Time!" Aunt Sylvia called after me as I was making a crazy dash for my bedroom.

Family Time was definitely not important at a time like this.

I picked up my favorite paintbrush. In my artist mind I saw my Uncle Ralph as a *real* movie star. I imagined him riding into the sunset as an enormous taco with a huge twirling mustache and a cowboy hat on his head. He'd be the most talented actor in the world. I saw him on the big screen. Lights, makeup, hair! Uncle Ralph, famous. And even if his acting didn't make him famous, my painting would.

As I painted, all of Uncle Ralph's funny voices rang through my head.

YEEEE-ha! TAAA-co, TAAA-co, chew it apart. Dog-eat-dog. Hut, hut! The show must go on. Ta-COOOO. Touchdown!

It wasn't so easy to get Uncle Ralph perfect in paint. It took me a long time, twenty minutes at least. At one point I had to paint over him with purple paint and start all over again.

Then came Aunt Sylvia. She had to be painted as really caring about teeth. And straight into my artist mind danced Aunt Sylvia with an enormous tooth for a head. Really, there was no other way to paint her. And it was a nice tooth head, white as snow and not a single cavity.

Holy moly—no, Monika, no! Toothbrush—thirty chews per—sweetie, sweetie, open up—plaque and cavities and—today it's teeth; tomorrow, no tee—

Her huge tooth head and her long and skinny toothbrush body were curled across the purple paper with Uncle Ralph. Yes, just like that. Aunt Sylvia looked perfect.

Of course Cousin Junior came into my mind as an alien in a shade of moldy green (I had to mix some paint—pukey yellow and outer-space blue—to get the color just right). He had large red antennae coming out of the thing that was supposed to be his head. On the front of his bumpy chest were the words "Planet Weirdo." The Art and History People would probably argue a lot about where he'd come from.

Beep-beep. Zam! Pow! Alien attack, alien attack, 94765, 94765. Come in, Control. Zing, zap—gotcha— beep-beep—*play, play, play*—

Painting Cousin Junior gave me a big headache, but finally his alien body was twisted and flying all over my paper. The perfect alien for all sorts of exciting missions.

Last of all, I painted a tiny purple Noonie Norton in the bottom corner. It would be my famous signature.

I stood back and looked at my work.

Brilliant.

Then I wrote a letter to my dad with my purple marker.

Dear Dad,

You should really come home PRONTO! I painted a brilliant masterpiece that's definitely going to make me famous. If you come back RIGHT NOW—for the Grover Cleveland Art Contest, I'll explain my painting to you in person so you don't have to read it in a book. In a hundred years.

Love,
Noonie

P.S. Aunt Sylvia and Uncle Ralph and Cousin Junior DID cure me. Sort of . . .

On the back of my letter I painted a purple picture of *me*, not a bit sick. Then I painted about a hundred bones all around me.

Georgia O'Keeffe is one of my very favorite artists in my *Masterpieces* book. She painted all sorts of bones. Bones and more bones from the desert. I was absolutely positive that Georgia O'Keeffe would have loved my painting. And my dad would love it too because he digs around for bones all the time.

Noonie Norton's bone painting was much better than any ol' yak bones.

I stuffed my painted letter inside the envelope.

Then I took my letter out again.

At the very bottom I wrote:

P.P.S. I hope you like your special presents.

I very carefully put one of my mom's purple postcards and the happy picture of the three of us inside the envelope. These special presents would definitely make him remember. Nothing else would matter but my masterpiece and me.

THE ARTIST AND ARTISTIC DIFFERENCES

Rrrrrrrring!

I didn't roll over and snort, and I didn't cover my face with my pillow. It was the third day of my Purple Period.

A very, very important day.

"*NOONIE!* Wakey-wakey, sweetie!" Aunt Sylvia opened my bedroom door. When she saw me, her eyes were bigger than eggs over easy. I was uppy-uppy already and out of bed. I had put on a very bright shirt that was less wrinkled; I had combed the knots out of my hair.

"Well," Aunt Sylvia chirped, "holy moly! Would you look at this? Noonie up and ready for school." Then she left to make breakfast as usual.

"This is it." I took my purple painting down from the easel and rolled it up. "My big debut!" I put my nose in the air and walked straight to the kitchen with artistic confidence.

Uncle Ralph was already sitting at the breakfast table in his mail uniform. Junior ran in and sat down next to him. Aunt Sylvia handed out the brown toast and sat next to Junior. I took a deep breath and stepped on top of my chair. This was a very important moment in my career, and I wanted them to pay close attention.

I cleared my throat and started my speech: "Introducing Noonie Norton's first painting exhibition. You are about to see the brilliant family painting *Masterpiece in Purple*, by the brilliant artist *Noonie Norton!*"

Then, very slowly, I unrolled my painting. I was sure they'd clap like crazy. Shouts and cheers. Bravo! *Magnifico!*

But that's not exactly what happened. Their mouths opened wide just like *The Scream.*

Silence.

Tick-tick-tick.

It seemed like a whole hour without a single word.

Finally Aunt Sylvia said, "Um—well . . . it's . . . *nice*." She scooted back in her chair.

"Nice?" I said.

"It's . . . pretty?" said Uncle Ralph, scrunching his face.

"*Pretty?*"

"It's . . . *scary!*" shouted Junior. He started making scary faces back at my painting.

Aunt Sylvia shushed him. Then she nervously pointed at my painting and asked, "Uh—sweetie? Is that supposed to be *me*?"

I smiled. "Yup. I know you care a whole lot about teeth!"

"Hmmm, well." Uncle Ralph itched his armpit. "I'll be darned. I sorta look like some sorta cowboy enchilada."

"You're a taco. And a *real* cowboy," I told him, getting just a little bit itchy. "A movie star."

"Ohhhh," said Uncle Ralph, rubbing his eyes.

"How come I look like a weirdo?" Cousin Junior whined with peanut butter and jelly all over his big mouth. He flung his cape over his chunky back.

"It's abstract," I told the three of them.

"But," said Aunt Sylvia, "I think there's something

wrong with my head." She was obviously very confused about abstract art.

Junior and Uncle Ralph stopped looking at themselves and turned their attention to Aunt Sylvia in my painting. Junior said, "That's not a head. It's a *tooth*!" He started to laugh and howl.

"By George, he's right, honey!" said Uncle Ralph. "You have a tooth for a head."

"*Tooth head! Tooth head!*" shouted Junior.

Aunt Sylvia had to breathe deep breaths and count to sixty. I thought she might cry, but instead she said, "At least I'm not some rope-toting cow patty!"

Uncle Ralph loved that one. He slapped his hand on the kitchen table and hollered "YEEEE-ha!" in his best cowboy voice.

Junior looked about ready to wet his pants. "*Cow patty! Cow patty!*" he crowed.

Aunt Sylvia and Uncle Ralph and Junior were laughing at each other until they all had tears in their eyes. It wasn't supposed to go like this.

"You—really—have—quite an imagination, sweetie!" chirped Aunt Sylvia, trying to catch her breath between her hysterical laughs.

My artistic confidence had disappeared. "It took

a—a lot of—careful thought. And feeling. I stared a lot, and I had artist's block, and I tried so many things to get you just . . . perfect."

But they were having so much fun that they barely heard me.

"It—it took a lot of very special *ar—ar—artist power*," I stuttered. "And you won't be mentioned in a single book," I squeaked. "When everyone writes about *me!*"

I looked at my painting. The tooth head and the twisted orange mustache and the alien antennae and the enormous taco cowboy definitely didn't look like a masterpiece. Not anymore. It was ugly art. Very, very ugly. And it made people laugh.

So I ripped it up.

Rip . . .

rip . . .

rip.

I threw the pieces in the air and watched them fall quietly like snow on top of Aunt Sylvia and Uncle Ralph and Cousin Junior. And finally they were quiet, too.

"Oh, sweetie," said Aunt Sylvia, "we weren't laughing at *you*."

"Maybe we just don't really understand it, Li'l Sport," said Uncle Ralph.

"Not a single bit," agreed Junior, shaking his head.

"Maybe you can try again?" suggested Aunt Sylvia. "Maybe you can paint something a bit more . . . normal? A happy family painting? Maybe?"

I sighed a big sigh. They wanted to be a perfect family in perfect lines. They'd never laugh at Sue Ann Pringle's painting. Suddenly I hollered like a famous crazy artist, "Of course you can't possibly understand my fine art and me! No one does!"

"But—" started Uncle Ralph, and Aunt Sylvia, and Cousin Junior.

I stomped my foot. "I'll have to go to Paris. Or to Rome. Or to China. Where brilliant artists are appreciated. You may never, ever see me again!" I looked each of them straight in the eye. "And then you'll miss me for sure."

the Artist's Practical Assistant

I lay down on the cold floor of my room and shut my eyes tight.

"I'm never going to paint again," I said to the ceiling. "I'd rather floss my teeth or comb my hair. I'd rather do math."

"Noonie?"

"I'd rather go to Grover Cleveland."

"Noonie?"

"I'd rather go to the hallway or to Principal Baloney's office," I said louder, sounding like a tragic soap opera star. "I'd rather be Sue Ann Pringle. Or a burrito. I'd rather do anything but paint."

"Was this your painting for the contest? It looks like your painting." The voice kept blabbing. "I have some tape, Noonie."

When I opened my eyes, there was a face staring at me. Reno. He always had an uncanny ability to show up at the wrong time. The pieces of my ripped painting were stuffed in the pressed pockets of his pants. He was holding a huge roll of tape that he just happened to carry around with him. His backpack was always filled with practical supplies. "We can put your painting back together again."

I sniffled. "I'm afraid not, Reno."

"But we have to. The school art contest is *today*!" Reno plunked himself down next to me and started trying to match my painting pieces like a puzzle. He stuck an alien antenna and a cowboy mustache together with Scotch tape.

"I'm afraid that I have way more important things to do."

I was going to throw all of my paints and paintbrushes in the trash. I was finally going to return my *Masterpieces* book to the Grover Cleveland library and rip up all my old rotten paintings. *Rip-rip-rip.* The sooner the better.

"More important than the art contest? But maybe I can help you. I'm your assistant, remember?"

"I think you're going to be late for school, Reno. For math and that stupid contest."

"Being a famous artist's assistant is *much* more important," Reno said with so much gusto that his glasses fell off. "I can tape your paintings together when you rip them up."

"No, Reno."

"I can hand you your brushes."

"Not necessary."

"I can clean your paint trays and mix your colors and steal your big soup cans and—"

"Why don't you go be Sue Ann Pringle's assistant?" I made my most dramatic pouty face. "She definitely needs artistic help."

"I don't want to be Sue Ann's assistant. I want to *help you.*"

"It's no use, Reno." I finally sat up. "It doesn't matter now. I'm not going to be an artist. It was just a lousy ol' painting."

"It's probably a *masterpiece!*" Reno stared at all the pieces on the floor.

"That's because you can't possibly understand what a *real artistic masterpiece* is."

Silence.

Suddenly Reno blubbered, "I'm good at something, too, Noonie! Just 'cause I'm not an *artist* doesn't mean that I'm not good at anything, Noonie! I'm the best at math and science in the whole school! I'm going to be a—a brilliant mathematician. Or a physicist."

"Boring, boring!" I shouted.

Reno stomped his foot with scientific temperament. He was so ruffled that his books fell straight out of his hands and back onto my floor.

He picked up his chemistry book. "I could be the next Einstein," he said in a huff, picking up *Theories on the Atom.* "Or the next Galileo or Edison! I might have books written about *me* in a hundred years!"

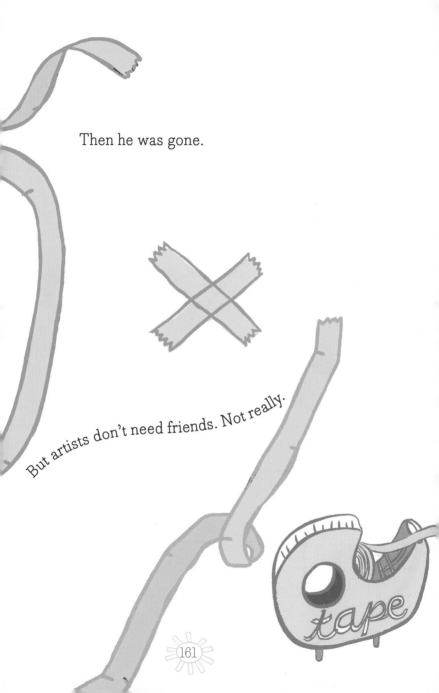

Then he was gone.

But artists don't need friends. Not really.

tape

chapter fourteen

THE ARTIST and HER FRIENDS

I was sadder than sad and bluer than blue. I was painfully purple.

No friends. No family. No painting. I'd never have the guts to show my face at Grover Cleveland. Never again. Ms. Lilly would have to say, "Well, that Noonie Norton did have quite a talent. A long, long time ago. If only she had *painted* something." Sue Ann Pringle would win the contest. Of course.

And my dad would have no real reason to fly home pronto.

I felt an exotic artist sickness coming on fast. Some sort of flu or pneumonia. Possibly warts.

I stayed there on my cold floor for who knows how long. At least a whole lot of minutes.

Tick-tick-tick.

Being a tragic artist takes a lot of time.

"Li'l Sport? May I come in?" Uncle Ralph knocked quietly on my bedroom door.

"No!" I hollered back. "Definitely not. I definitely need to be *alone*."

Aunt Sylvia was outside my door, too. "Sweetie? Are you—"

"I am very, very sick!" I cried. "I'm so sick that I won't be able to go to school. Ever again. And you definitely can't cure me."

I heard Aunt Sylvia breathe a deep breath. She must've stayed home from her tooth job. I heard Uncle Ralph pacing back and forth and Junior bawling that he was sick like me, so he should skip morning kindergarten.

"Do you wanna play, Noonie?" he said between sniffles outside my door. "I'll take you prisoner again if you want. That'll make you feel better."

"Go away!" I shouted to Junior. "Go away! Go away!" I shouted to the three of them.

And finally they did.

I barely had the energy to reach over for my artist suitcase. I barely had the strength to pull out my *Masterpieces* book. I opened it as the pages flipped and fluttered. Artists' faces flashed by, and so did their masterpieces. The famous artists were just about the only ones left who'd understand everything. Along with my mom.

And then . . .

Frida Kahlo came in a bright tropical flurry with all of her Mexican monkeys and butterflies. She made her way straight to my bed. Vincent van Gogh looked windblown and scrappy from wandering all over the place. Edvard Munch appeared in a cloud of black and gray. He disappeared, then reappeared and tried to hide like a shadowy figure in the corner.

Andy Warhol and Jean-Michel Basquiat were already arguing about important statements. Somehow all sorts of graffiti artists had snuck in with them, and they were hip-hopping and rap-rapping and eyeing my big white wall. Georgia O'Keeffe was there too, and Jackson Pollock, who was practically covered in paint splotches and tracking paint all over my floor.

The famous artists were drinking coffee from tiny cups, and their messy hair was flying in a million directions under their artist hats.

From the floor I tried to look over their tall heads for my mom. I was sure she had to be in my room somewhere. She was a famous artist, too. Or she should've been very, very famous.

But I couldn't find her.

The other artists set their artist suitcases down. They looked down at me, tilting their heads one way, and then the other.

They scratched their chins. This was very serious.

"Oh, my," said Vincent van Gogh.

"Oh, dear," said Frida Kahlo, shaking her bed head.

"What a pity," said Georgia O'Keeffe.

"A pitiful purple pity," emphasized Edvard Munch.

"I remember when I was like that." Basquiat pointed down at me.

"Ah, yes," agreed all the famous artists, sadly nodding.

"Those were awfully sour days," said Munch.

"Nasty, lousy, rotten days," said Kahlo.

I sat up. They understood. "My painting!" I cried like a soap opera star. "Did you hear what they said?"

"We heard," said the artists as they elbowed one another and crowded for space in my tiny bedroom.

"They laughed at me!" I hollered passionately.

"Those nincompoops!" barked Jackson Pollock, scrunching his wrinkled forehead. He shook himself like a wet dog, and paint drops splattered the graffiti artists. But they didn't care.

"Everyone's a critic!" spat Andy Warhol, almost making his funny wig fall off.

"Chew-chew-chewing everything apart!" snorted Georgia O'Keeffe as she fiddled with some bones.

"The masses never appreciate fine art." Van Gogh covered his missing ear.

"They may eventually, but they always laugh at first," said Edvard Munch.

"You mean, they laughed at you too?" I asked in a tiny voice.

"Yes. Oh, yes," replied Munch.

"But of course." Frida Kahlo fluffed my pillow and looked at herself in a pocket mirror. She twitched her black eyebrows, which looked just like a black crow's wings.

"You'll get used to it," added Basquiat, tossing his dreadlocks.

"I sold only one painting in my entire life," mumbled Vincent van Gogh, looking quite depressed as he itched his elbow through one of the holes in his shirt. "They all said I was crazy."

"He *was* crazy." The famous artists nodded.

"You even ate your paint," I added.

"Yes, well." Van Gogh turned to me with a little spark lighting up his crazy eyes. "Art is life, and life is art. And a brilliant artist never quits."

Never quits? I wasn't sure. Not sure at all.

But the famous artists were sure. They suddenly *had* to do their art. All over my bedroom.

Basquiat jumped up from the floor. There were

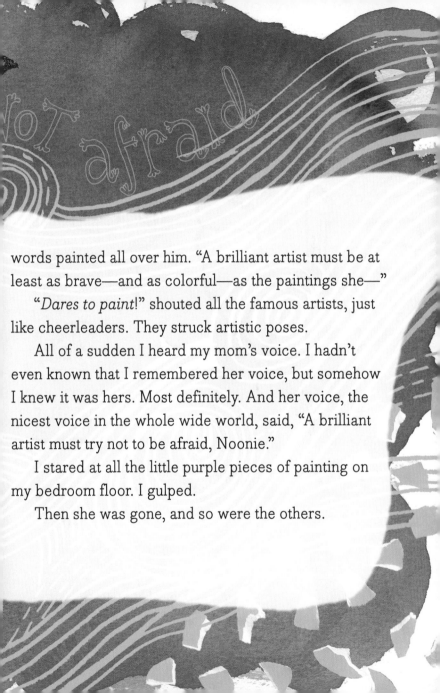

words painted all over him. "A brilliant artist must be at least as brave—and as colorful—as the paintings she—"

"*Dares to paint!*" shouted all the famous artists, just like cheerleaders. They struck artistic poses.

All of a sudden I heard my mom's voice. I hadn't even known that I remembered her voice, but somehow I knew it was hers. Most definitely. And her voice, the nicest voice in the whole wide world, said, "A brilliant artist must try not to be afraid, Noonie."

I stared at all the little purple pieces of painting on my bedroom floor. I gulped.

Then she was gone, and so were the others.

The Artists Surprise about Prizes

Ms. Lilly was hanging the last painting
in the smelly gymnasium. There were so
many families hanging on the wall. Some
paintings had dogs or cats or gerbils. Some
had one parent, and others seemed to have
a hundred. There were stick people that
looked just like cave paintings and some
paintings with no people at all.

But none of the paintings looked quite
like mine.

"Noonie, I'm so glad you made it!" Ms.
Lilly smiled and gave me a little hug as I
walked in out of breath. "I knew you would."

Actually I'd barely made it. I'd spent the whole morning taping my painting back together again. Then, I brilliantly escaped from my relatives' house without Aunt Sylvia noticing and wildly dashed to Grover Cleveland. Just in time.

Ms. Lilly took my painting and unrolled it and thumbtacked it in place.

I swear my painting practically came alive on the wall!

It looked as if Uncle Ralph, with his huge cowboy hat and his twisted mustache, and Aunt Sylvia, with her giant tooth head, and Cousin Junior, with his alien antennae, were all *right there*. All tangled up in a jumbled mishmash. They looked even more original since I had ripped them up and taped them together.

"Wow," said Ms. Lilly, which I interpreted to mean that she was shocked by the twisted beauty of it. "What a painting, Noonie."

"Thanks, Ms. Lilly." I smiled as I set my artist suitcase down and sat underneath my painting.

Reno, who hadn't even painted anything for the art contest, was pretending to look at other paintings, but he was actually looking at mine. I was sure of it. When he saw me, though, he put his nose high in the air and tripped over a toddler.

Meanwhile, the families circled the gym. When people got to my painting, they scrunched their eyes and itched their chins. Kids pointed at the tooth head, or the taco movie star, or the alien boy. One baby just wrinkled up his tiny face and wailed.

But I didn't care. Sometimes art makes people uncomfortable; it might make babies cry. I was absolutely positive that my dad would understand if he'd been at the contest to see my brilliant painting hanging on the wall.

I stared at the gymnasium floor.

I waited.

No dad. No mom.

No one.

Then I saw Principal Baloney pull out the prize-winning ribbons! I leaped up from the floor and sprinted across the gym and practically knocked right into him.

"Whoaaa. Well, look who's here. Miss Noonie Norton." Principal Baloney let out a hearty chuckle and gave me a pat on the back.

"Hi, Principal Baloney. I mean Principal Maloney. Guess what? I actually did my homework," I said, bouncing up and down. "My homework for art class."

"Isn't that something? Good for you, Noonie." He hung up the first honorable mention ribbon and looked down at me. "See? Maybe school isn't so bad. Maybe it's a good thing you haven't left the country."

Principal Baloney put up another honorable mention ribbon. And then another. Families clapped and winners beamed. Hmmph. The honorable mention paintings had absolutely no originality. No imagination at all. Boring, boring.

"Well, my dad should be coming any second now!" I jogged to keep up with Principal Baloney. "Then we'll take off. As soon as he sees my painting. As soon as—"

Principal Baloney tacked up a large yellow ribbon: third place. The sixth-grader hugged his parents and his little sister. Someone snapped a photo. *Snap-snap.* A happy-family picture.

There was a trail of people following Principal Baloney and me. Everyone wanted to see who had won the art contest.

Second place.

First place.

176

Principal Baloney's feet stopped right in front of my painting. He fidgeted with the ribbons. He squinted at my painting, and he undoubtedly saw my famous signature. I swear his lips curled up: a tiny little smile. He was obviously amazed by my homework, my brilliant work of art.

"Good job, Noonie." Principal Baloney patted my head. "It looks as though you put a lot of hard work into your painting."

"Yes," I sputtered. "I did." My heart was about to fly out of my chest, and my knees were shaking like crazy. I was practically having a terrible fourth-grade art attack. "A whole lot of work."

And then . . . Principal Baloney walked straight past my painting and back across the gym to Sue Ann's painting. I saw his large hand go up, and so did the red ribbon.

There was clapping, but I barely noticed, and Sue Ann didn't seem to notice either. "Thanks," she said, sort of shrugging. She wasn't even smiling or giggling. "It's nothing, really."

The masses moved on, and Sue Ann was left sitting all by herself underneath her painting. Quiet tears were running down her not-so-perfect face.

I was so shocked to see Sue Ann Pringle crying that I didn't chase after Principal Baloney, and I didn't sniffle a single bit when he tacked up the biggest blue ribbon on a kindergartner's painting. Basically a bunch of scribbles.

Reno was still standing in front of Sue Ann's painting. I pretended not to see him, and he pretended not to see me.

"Congratulations, Sue Ann," said Reno. "I like your painting."

"Thanks, Reno." She was looking down at her lap and chipping her polished fingernails. "It doesn't really matter."

Finally I got a good look at Sue Ann Pringle's painting.

She was smack in the center.

I could tell it was her because the

girl had yellow curls and was wearing a pink dress. But the Sue Ann Pringle in the painting didn't look happy. Not happy at all. Her mouth was a jaggedy pink squiggle. A mom was far off on one side, and a dad was way, way over on the other side. Only a little brown dog sat at Sue Ann's painted feet, with pink ribbons around its ears.

I stared and stared at it. Then I stared at Sue Ann. "Um—is that your mom?"

"Yeah, she lives kind of far away now. My dad still lives here." Sue Ann tapped her perfectly white tennis shoes together. "And that's my dog, Sparkles. He gets to go with me to both houses."

"You have two houses?"

"Yeah. I'm going to start spending summers at my mom's house and the school year at my dad's house. It's kind of weird."

"But then who's that?" asked Reno, squinting his eyes and pointing almost straight up.

There was a tiny little person in the corner of Sue Ann's painting. I thought it was supposed to be her again, her signature, but—

"Oh, that's my stepmom. She just got married to my dad about a month ago."

The three of us were quiet.

The janitor dragged in his bucket and his mop. He was ready to mop up the gymnasium floor. Principal Baloney was standing by the door and saying good-bye to the happy families. Students from Grover Cleveland were extra happy because we all had the rest of the day off. All because of the art contest.

"Well," said Sue Ann, standing up and brushing off her pink dress. "I guess that's it."

"Yeah, I guess that's it," I agreed. The gymnasium was almost empty. "Sue Ann, are your parents—I mean, aren't any of them, here? At the art contest?"

"Nah. My dad is out of town for business." Sue Ann took down her painting and started to roll it up. "And my stepmom? I told her not to come. I didn't want her to come."

I nodded. Reno awkwardly shuffled his feet and fiddled with the calculator in his pocket.

"I guess there's always next year," sighed Sue Ann, picking up her flowery lunch box filled with art supplies.

I sighed, too. "Yeah, there's always next year."

chapter sixteen

The Artist's Appreciation

I slowly walked back to my painting and sat down.

I set my artist suitcase right in front of me and put my elbows on top of it. I blew my messy hair out of my eyes and adjusted my artist hat.

"I *love* your painting, Noonie."

I looked up from the floor. Ms. Lilly sat down next to me.

"It's very brave. And so colorful!"

"Thanks." I really wanted to believe Ms. Lilly. "But it didn't win. Not a single thing."

"No. But you and I know that doesn't matter. Vincent van Gogh sold only one painting—"

"In his whole short life. I know."

"Well, I hope you keep painting, Noonie. You have so much talent."

I tried to pull my artist hat down over my face. "Guess I get it from my mom."

"Noonie," Ms. Lilly said softly. "Reno told me about your mom."

"My mom?" I choked out. That Reno. Nosy, nosy. Why couldn't he mind his own—

"That must be so sad for you," continued Ms. Lilly in her nice voice. "And now, with your dad gone sometimes—"

"He should be coming back, though." I flipped through the pages of my *Masterpieces* book, pretending to look at famous art. "Any second now."

"I'm sure he'll be back as soon as he can. And I'm sure he's so proud of you." Ms. Lilly looked up at my painting again.

I took a deep breath. "Ms. Lilly, do you think people will ever like my art? I mean, even in a hundred years? I know that my mom would love my paintings. And I'm pretty sure that all the famous artists would love my paintings, too. Because they'd understand everything. And my dad collects all my work just because he's my dad. But—"

"*People* already do, Noonie." Ms. Lilly smiled her very kind smile. "I do. You don't have to wait a hundred years. I like your art right now."

I scrunched my face and sniffled. And then I told Ms. Lilly everything. I had to tell someone, and Ms. Lilly was the perfect person. She wasn't a normal person; she was an artist. I told her about my Blue Period and my first self-portrait. I told her that I couldn't decide whether I was "better off" living with Aunt Sylvia and Uncle Ralph, my temporary family, or traveling with my dad. All over the world. I told her about my mom, who'd been a brilliant artist, too, even though I couldn't remember her so well. I told her about my mom's Purple Period. And mine. I opened my artist suitcase and showed Ms. Lilly the paints my mom had left for me, and her postcards, and the napkin inside my artist hat.

Ms. Lilly looked at them as if she were studying famous art. As if she were in a famous gallery in Paris or in Rome. She listened very carefully to everything about my blue and purple life. She nodded sometimes, and sometimes she said "hmmm" or "ohhhh."

Finally I stopped talking. We were both quiet. Then I shrugged and said, "I guess I have to remember my mom through her paints." I put my hand on my red artist suitcase. "And her paintings." I took off my artist hat and ran my finger along the wild purple lines and curves on my mom's brilliant napkin.

"That's a really nice way to remember her, Noonie. I'm sure your mom would love to be remembered that way." Ms. Lilly slowly traced the little picture of my purple mom on the napkin. "Your mom was a talented artist, too."

Somehow the mysterious deadly lump in my throat was starting to go away. "I know," I practically whispered.

Ms. Lilly, the best art teacher in the whole world, stood up from the gymnasium floor and gently held out her hand to me. "Would you like a lift home?"

"Well," I answered, looking at my feet. "Um— I'm still . . . sort of waiting for someone, but—"

"I'm giving Sue Ann a ride. Why

don't you come with us? I think we're going to stop for ice cream."

Ice cream! Triple chocolate chunk!

Sue Ann Pringle, who didn't even care if she won a prize in the art contest, walked across the gym toward us, with her sad painting rolled up under her arm. She stood next to Ms. Lilly and stared at my painting. I could tell she was seriously studying it, undoubtedly thinking it was very funny. Or very messy.

"Your painting's really original, Noonie," Sue Ann suddenly said. "I think it was probably the most interesting painting in the contest. And I really like all the purple."

I looked straight at Sue Ann and tilted my head. Then I barely squeaked, "Thank you."

"So is that your family?"

"Well." I cleared my throat. "Yeah, kind of."

With artistic confidence, I stood up so I could point at my painting with my purple marker.

"This is my Aunt Sylvia. She *loves* teeth, see. Because she's very hygienic, and she doesn't want all of my teeth to fall out. She calls me sweetie even though she doesn't like me to eat sweets. But I don't really care because she gave me purple postcards painted by my mom. And my Uncle Ralph here? He's going to be a famous actor someday. That's why he works so hard playing a talented taco, even if the arts biz is definitely dog-eat-dog. This is my Cousin Junior, flying all over. He pretends to keep the world safe. And even if he captures artist prisoners, at least he buys my paintings.

"I've lived with them since kindergarten, and we always have boring Family Time, so I guess they're sort of, well, my family. For now, at least. Temporarily. Until my dad comes home."

And then a very unusually unusual thing happened. Something very artistically strange.

TOOTH

DOG EAT DOG

chapter seventeen

The Artist's Temp Family

Standing right in front of me wasn't my dad, but it *was* my temporary family.

"Oh, boy," said Uncle Ralph without any of his funny acting voices. "Did we miss the contest?" He was wearing his rumpled suit and a checked tie. Very unusual.

Junior wasn't wearing his superhero cape. He was almost acting like any human boy. No video game noises, no food on his face, no tantrums on the floor.

Aunt Sylvia wasn't wearing her crispy-clean dental-hygienist uniform or her squeaky white shoes. The art contest was obviously a very important occasion. She looked at my painting and tilted her head. "It's an awfully white tooth head. I can sure say that."

Uncle Ralph scratched his chin. "It's a very dramatic taco cowboy, that's for sure."

Junior came straight up to my painting and tried to zap the alien boy with his superhero finger—"*zap-zap-zing!*"—which I interpreted to mean that he liked himself now, sort of, as an alien.

"We felt so bad that you ripped up your painting, sweetie." Aunt Sylvia looked sad.

"Your painting of . . . *us*." Uncle Ralph puffed out his chest. I think he kind of liked seeing himself as art on the wall.

"*Rip-rip-rip!*" shouted Junior.

"We know you worked hard on it," continued Aunt Sylvia, "and then we upset you, and you didn't have anything for the art contest, and—"

"We thought you'd *quit*!" hollered Cousin Junior.

"No," I gulped. "An artist never quits."

"Well, that's exactly what Reno told us when he called," said Uncle Ralph, fiddling with his orange mustache. "When you weren't in your room, we came as fast as we could."

Aunt Sylvia nodded. "Reno said that as your assistant, he'd known you would make it here."

My head jerked around until I saw Reno. He was pretending to figure out math equations in his math book, but I knew he was listening.

"Darn good work, Li'l Sport!" Uncle Ralph put his arm around me in a big squeeze.

"We're very proud of you," said Aunt Sylvia.

"That painting is freaky," cried Junior, which I interpreted to mean that he thought it was very brave. And daring. He was putting his hands all over my painting, but I didn't really care.

Uncle Ralph cleared his throat. "We—uh—may not understand art so well, Li'l Sport. We try, but we're just not . . . Art People or anything. Like you."

I stared at my feet. "That's okay," I practically whispered.

"And now, sweetie, guess what?" Aunt Sylvia's eyes lit up, and she finally smiled her big white smile as she cheered, "It's time for ice cream!"

Uncle Ralph and Junior cheered too. "*Yee-HAAAA!*" yodeled Uncle Ralph as he patted his belly. "Let's celebrate!"

My eyes grew enormous, and I practically drooled.

"Oh," Aunt Sylvia turned to me and said, "unless you're still feeling sick."

"Sick? Me?" I bounced up and down in my tennis shoes. I started taking my masterpiece off the wall as fast as I could. "I feel perfectly perfect."

Then Junior ran around the gym making superhero noises while Uncle Ralph and Aunt Sylvia talked to Ms. Lilly and Sue Ann. I was sure they were all talking about me having quite a talent. And about going out for ice cream.

Reno was pretending to look at paintings on the wall, but mine was the only one left.

"Reno?" I said. He looked around as if he were hearing a mysterious ghost. Even though Reno was practically blind, he could definitely see me. "Reno?" I said again as he played with his calculator. "I just want you to know that—that—" I stuttered. "Well, that math is probably not *that* boring. It's just that—well, I'm not very good at—"

Reno suddenly opened his chemistry book and took out a piece of paper from the very back. It fell to the ground, right by my artist suitcase, and I picked it up. It was a paint-by-numbers; it was a normal painted girl with a big yellow sun. But on top of the girl's head he had painted a purple artist hat. It was a painting of—*me*! At least I think it was supposed to be me.

I carefully put it in the back of my *Masterpieces* book, with all my other paintings. "Thanks, Reno. You really have quite a talent with numbers."

Reno looked at his feet and played with his fingers. He pushed his glasses back up on his nose.

"And you're a pretty good artist's assistant too. You're very good at stealing paper bags and soup cans. And not letting me quit. So . . ." I squirmed. "I mean, if you still want to be my assistant, well—"

"Sure!" said Reno, cracking his big funny smile. "But Noonie? Can we still do math homework too? Maybe you can be my assistant."

I sighed.

Reno and I could never stay mad at each other for very long, even if he *was* a Math Person.

"Do you wanna get ice cream with us?" I asked. And he nodded like crazy.

I finished rolling up my painting and stuck it under my arm. Uncle Ralph held one of my hands, and Junior held the other. I was smooshed like a hamburger patty, but I didn't mind.

THE ArtIST AND ALL SORTS OF OTHER ArtISTS

I'd thought that Ice Cream Time counted as Family Time.

But no.

"*Sweetie!* Guess what?" cried Aunt Sylvia, as soon as we walked in our front door. "Tonight we're having Family Time in . . . *the family room!*"

Family Time in the family room?

I groaned. I imagined celery sticks and learning how to properly floss our teeth. I imagined jumping jacks and fiber and board games. I imagined all of us sitting on the striped couch together: one big family.

"But—" I squeaked.

"No big buts or little buts!" interrupted Aunt Sylvia, which made Junior crack up like crazy.

And me? I made a wild dash for my bedroom, clutching my red artist suitcase. I definitely didn't have time for Family Time.

I had very important things to do.

I was probably going to stay up all night painting.

I had to study my *Masterpieces* book, which I was never going to return to the Grover Cleveland library. The famous artists probably never won grade school art contests. It was probably a very good sign that I hadn't won.

I looked around my room for the famous artists with their tiny coffee cups and their suitcases. I looked for Frida in my bed and shadowy Edvard Munch in my corner. I looked for drippy Jackson Pollock and the hiding graffiti artists and Georgia O'Keeffe with her bones. And I looked for my mom.

But it was just me.

"Li'l Sport? Are you comin' out to help us?" called Uncle Ralph from the family room.

"Holy moly, sweetie!" called Aunt Sylvia. "We're making a mess of things out here!"

A mess? I was curious. So I opened my bedroom door and tiptoed down the hallway and peeked into the family room.

Aunt Sylvia and Uncle Ralph and Cousin Junior were all painting. I squinted my eyes and tilted my head. I was trying very hard to interpret their work, but their paintings were the most abstract things I'd ever seen.

Uncle Ralph seemed to have a very bad case of artist's block: he was pacing back and forth, talking in various voices to his painting with a jagged frown. Junior definitely had a case of *The Scream*. He was finger-painting and getting googley splotches of paint all over everything. His mouth hung open against his chunky chin like a big screamy O. Aunt Sylvia had some sort of exotic painting sickness. She was sighing a lot, and her big hair drooped.

They all desperately needed help from a brilliant artist.

I took a deep breath and counted to thirty. And then I started to giggle. Just a little. Because artists can be very, very funny. "Bravo," I said to myself. "*Magnifico*." And I walked straight into the family room.

chapter
nineteen

The Artist
on Artistic Endings

Dear Art and History People,

Today is the end of my Purple Period.

Please pay close attention and take a lot of notes.

It went just like this: I had a very famous art exhibit in a very famous gallery.

Well, it wasn't exactly famous. Ms. Lilly was there, and Reno, and even Sue Ann came with her dad and her stepmom. They wanted to see my brilliant work—*and* the original paintings by the other artists in our family room: Aunt Sylvia, Uncle Ralph, and Junior. We'd stayed up nearly all night painting. Well, at least until nine o'clock.

My new painting was *quite* a masterpiece.

It looked like this: Tropical butterflies flew around my purple wavy sky while monkeys climbed on yak blobs and an Edvard Munch scream face. A bunch of Frida Kahlo black-crow eyebrows and all sorts of Vincent van Gogh ears flapped all over the place. Reno was wearing new glasses, and Aunt Sylvia, Uncle Ralph, and Cousin Junior were wearing artist hats. A laughing Ms. Lilly sat on top of a beat-up artist car, and my dad was flying home. But best of all, I was smack in the center, and my mom was way up high, looking down at me. Smiling.

In the books about me you'll have to include all the people in this last purple painting. Then you'll be able to figure everything out in a hundred years.

After the art exhibit I walked straight to the mail-box, with Reno tagging along as usual. And *guess what*? There wasn't just a letter inside, but a package! Sent by express mail. Very, very important. And sure enough, it was addressed to me: *Noonie Norton*! It had scribbly letters on it in some foreign language and a funny-looking stained stamp.

Dear Noonie,

I'm so happy that your serious mysterious sicknesses are cured. Your Aunt Sylvia told me. She also told me about the art contest at Grover Cleveland. I was on my way home as a surprise because I really wanted to see your painting! Unfortunately, my plane got delayed in Hong Kong, and my luggage got lost in South Africa. My bus broke down in Egypt, and I ended up trudging across the desert. But just my luck! In the desert I happened to discover the fossil of a cave cockroach! It's a long story.

"A creepy crunchy cockroach?" I said to Reno. He shrugged as I kept reading.

Now I'm at the airport in Greece, and I should be home in just a couple of days. To see YOU. And your masterpiece.

"A couple of days?" I screamed to Reno. That's practically any second now! It worked, Reno! See? My artist power worked!"

In the meantime, I've sent a very special present so you'll remember me. And your mom. I miss you!
Love,
Dad

P.S. Did I ever tell you that your mom had a Polka-Dot Period?

And there in the
package I found something
much better than a mummy or a
cockroach in a cave. I couldn't believe it!
It was a *polka-dot* scarf, all the way from
Greece!

WOW

Of course I had to put my new scarf around my
neck immediately. I had to, even if it hung down to my
knees. Most likely I will never take my polka-dot artist
scarf off ever again.

Because my dad also sent me a
map of the world, all folded up. On the back
of the map was a self-portrait painted by my mom
a long, long time ago. Her polka-dot painting. Brilliant.

I took off my purple Chinese artist hat and laid it in
my suitcase, right on top of my *Masterpieces* book.
I snapped my suitcase shut.

Because today, Art and History People, is the beginning of my Polka-Dot Period.

Make a note.

My Polka-Dot Period will undoubtedly be even
better than my Purple Period. I'm sure of it.

Sincerely

noonie
norton